STANDARD DREAMING

STANDARD
DREAMING

by Hortense Calisher

ARBOR HOUSE

NEW YORK

Library of Congress Catalog Card Number: 72-82176
ISBN 0-87795-043-1

Manufactured in the United States of Amercia

Second Printing, 1972

STANDARD DREAMING

AT six o'clock on the evening of the last Friday in the past July, Dr. Berners tells us, he reentered his office here in the hospital after reattaching the severed hand of an accident victim, and stood before the window, as is his habit when recovering his nonsurgery self. Thinking as well of this report. To calibrate a parent is not easy. So much of it is not parenthood. He decides to put everything in.

Midsummers around that time, he could watch the city changeover telegraph itself west-east from river to river—the New York invitation, or threat—in his blood ever since his early teens and first visit here, as one freshly arrived boy-vegetable, opal-cheeked and cocoa-calm, from Switzerland. In winters, the office light goes from bluebell to dark; then only he thought of his alp-ringed childhood, the neat prunings around his father's dispensary, and air like a carillon breathed.

This night, the window was letting in a heat-roughened rosiness already browning at the edges, with less than usual hints of golden goings-on elsewhere. The weekend buzz outside was a leaving one. Technically sundown, nighttime for the single here. All this would loom large in such a report.

Over his secretary's rounded back, he saw on his desk a bowl of fresh lichee nuts; half his patients were now from Chinatown, almost all of his practice being now through this hospital.

"Lichee light," he said—he always says something—and reaches over for one of the nuts, fondling its cobbled, inflamed brown—not wood, not bark, not skin. "That sky."

She doesn't answer, hasn't in eighteen years. The Swiss, with some of the best climate in Europe, are its worst weather bores; on his first working return there after a war he had served as surgeon in, he and his French wife had met in Vevey, on just that note. "They try to be such artists about it," she'd said, taking him for an American. "A boring people generally," he told her. "All Europe thinks so—and we know." Stoically he and they suffered their median selves. Even when they were handsome—like *you*, Renee said—there was seldom enough flash for one to notice it, and like pigs fed on chestnut, she said, their flesh had no rankness; some early ozone kept their linen fresher than other peoples'

even when they emigrated, and maybe their souls too—
how could she have mistaken him for anything else!
"Your kisses taste of camomile." He had chewed tablets,
as he had observed doctors there did before examining
—since he had never before had a private patient, or a
female one. A courtesy to his superior, whose niece she
was—a wart removal, from the delicate cheek, tiny
lobe. None on the pointed tongue. Sex mixed with the
surgery, even when sliding honorably into marriage,
was maybe unlucky; all that esprit, boring to him in
the end though he never told her so, had carried her
off early, leaving him free again to be a monk for
medicine. But a father.

He never missed her sharply, except when he went up
to Boston. To stand in that slum alley, first locking the
car against the idlers there—maybe they're not stealers,
but they stare at it and him as at a Trojan horse—and
look up at the blind windows of that hermit second
story, readying himself. To abase himself, before his
son.

He strips a lichee and pops the pure, slippery oval in
his mouth. More and more he has a taste for what he
thinks of as forest nourishment. "Who brought?"

"Mei-ling's mother."

That half-formed little fist will never be a beauty, but
the new operating rotunda here, in the American style,
almost as large as an amphitheater, is full of students, and

of us doctors, too, every time he works on it. Reminding him that after his war service, his work with a surgeon's group, the Society of the Hand, was what had started him on a vanity practice. What are the decent limits of vanity in a human body, he asks us now? At what ridgeback of hair, daily callous of misery, horn of deformity, may it start? Or must it stop.

Erna the secretary, with him since the beginning, hands him a Kleenex for the juice on his fingers, then a pen and some checks, including one for the rent of the Park Avenue office, which he signs, Niels Berners, without flourish. "Guess I better give up the uptown office." Where patients seldom called anymore, never finding him there. "Hadn't I, hmm?" Answers Erna never gave. But he would feel her approval if he had it. He didn't. "What, no tea today?"

She brings him his cup of a brew called Constant Comment, a tin of which his son had once sent him from Cambridge, as a joke. Awesome to recall that he once had a Harvard son, and a joke with him.

"Guess I'm hooked on this stuff." He says this everyday too. To please her? Stichmain, god of orthopedics at his former hospital, maintained that a daily ounce of ritual was just the placebo to keep the lower staff satisfied. Strange to think of that thick-skinned muscle-guesser (whose daughter, rumor says, now has her own kind of habit) as only another beaten father. Drugs no longer seem to Berners the worst. Rather—incurably simpler. A mass placebo, even when a child—or a parent —dies of them. He admits that if his own only child took drugs he mightn't see as clearly that the parent-child disease is larger, must be something else. Still, there is Stichmain, one more member of the son-blasted, daughter-bitten Society of the Child.

"Where'd you get that tea these days, Erna? Altman's?"

"Mail order."

She knows what he's hooked on. He's touched. And brusque to it. "Okay, see you in two weeks. Have a good time on the Cape May, with the mam*mah*. And take with you that box over there."

When he sees her redden with pleasure at the perfume and the stole—which will she give to the mammah?—he wants to spirit her upstairs, quick under the arc lights, to lift the sad, virginal forehead, that meek jowl, even those unused breasts—an operation which he now will do for no one—and then? What surgical correction is there for mother-monkey on the back?

At once he reports himself to himself. Old thinking! Which, who knows, may have its quiet victims lying in state in every mortuary in the nation, under every diagnosis but the true? In the parentism produced by the Society of the Child, one never blames the child. Still, having seen that mood-sucking Viennese monkey,

Mrs. Krants, he finds it hard to blame poor Erna, who at the heights of her mother's candy-eating dependency is still called *"Lump!"* Yet there must be something. Erna is a child, in every house and mortuary the unalterable love-object. Under the terms of the parents' group which he has been attending all winter, Dr. Berners reminds himself of what he is committed to hold fast to at every corner. A child is blameable. Raoul, up there behind the blind windows in his ashram of one— is a child.

He puts down his cup; he has finished it. Its gall is still sweet. "Okay, then—the answering service knows where I am tonight?"

"I gave them all the numbers. You didn't say where for tonight."

"Tonight we meet at Mrs. Hunter's."

Erna, who has met Baba Hunter, must be the only person who doesn't make a face at the mention of her. Holding fast at the corners for Baba isn't easy. But this is where the parents' group comes in. He goes out into that city musk, not single any more. To help Baba Hunter with her blame. Which presumably helps him with his.

"Good night."

"Good night, Doctor. And please remember, if you need me back sooner, just call."

As he closes the door, she is trying on the stole.

Outside, he recalls that when Raoul was little, he and Erna used to exchange postcards. And take trips to the zoo. In her mind, she is a mother to him. It never stops. She would get on my back if she could. With him.

Going up to Harlem via the East River Drive, he drove on past his goal to a spot just south of the Willis Avenue Bridge, one of those places here that he always says no one but foreigners ever see. He and Raoul used to collect them. He parked the car in a cul-de-sac off the Drive and walked back. Opposite him is an oval of green, oddly undusky shore, on which are two old, curved trees, wineglass elms or the next best; a pair of black boys are gamboling across it, but it is Gainsborough nevertheless. If the river running beneath were cloth instead of water, it would be of that kind once brought to kings, still to be seen in that arras under glass in the *musée* at Edam, or in the painted riverstreak under a saint's prow in the town hall at Siena. The finest eel-gray, dirty, iridescent—what was the name of that cloth in which kings used to clothe themselves? It bothers him, this interpenetration of everything, which people got out of easy by calling "culture." When he can't remember the name of the cloth, he gets in the car again and drives back slowly, past that high-rise mortuary of state madness, Manhattan State Hospital. Anybody passing it, who does not cry out, is to blame. At that point he remembers—samite! Raoul, in the eighth-grade pageant. Raoul, in a hospital ten years later, in dirty-gray menswear samite.

At that point Dr. Berners warns us. Beware the mind, young or old anywhere, that seeks an architectural peace for itself. It will cry out. He reminds himself that this is a full report.

He eats dinner in the No Name Restaurant near Baba's, Soul Food Served Here, Your Host—White Sambo, who proves to be an octoroon, that hot mauve color of the proudflesh round a healing wound. Berners is alone in the conversation pit where the tables are, and the ghosts of the Beatles in that pit in *Help!* If violence should come, aiming for money or color, he is in a straight bead from the door. Ideas aren't illusory and veiled anymore, rivers either. Yet what is wrong with him, that without logic, he still wants life? The soul food is fine, but he can't eat. His son is like a plummet of stone in the grave of his chest. This is the evening devoted to thoughts of him.

The owner, who has seen him and the group here, brings him coffee he says is made with eggshells in a granite pot. Berners drinks it, swallowing hard. *Essen sie Seele. Mangez de l'âme, Raoul.* Eat! Eat mine.

"Summin' wrah-ung food."

"My son. He starves."

"Uh-uh! Wo' prisoner?"

He can only shake his head.

"Uh . . ." Then that indescribable common sound, expelled from the catgut of the throat, like spittle. The owner looks about him tallying—white leathers, marble pit, soul. The mauve eyelids flutter. "Won't take yo' munnah."

"Nobody's."

Berners goes to the washroom and returns. He has wept.

The owner is waiting, that pleading look on his face. Toss him a bone.

"He is rejecting the world," Berners says. "And I shall die of it."

Berners wishes to add he is almost sure that, reverting to his childhood training under the Protestant Fathers of Berne, he said that last in Latin.

It is answered.

"I keep that table. Fo' you an' him. An' me an' mine."

Payment is refused.

———————◆———————

Beyond is his car, on the hood of which four small boys sit. They are about eight, the age of Mei-ling. Their eyes are the same velvet glass, their small nostrils and lips carved in the same shared substance which keeps all of them alike for a time. Berners looks closer. At one of them. What a surgeon knows best and before all techniques, he reminds us, is the look of the successive stages of flesh. In sickness and in health. His mind is married to it. Is it deeper than fancy that in this one the cornea already itches; the maze of a twofold torture is ready to bud behind that thought-scabied eye?

"Have you a mumma and dadda?" The child turns down the corners of his little frog-mouth. Berners swears to himself there is a spatial knowledge in the smile.

"Mumma."

In time, Berners is now ready to believe, the child and she will die of it.

Berners is in other words—new and dangerous words —ready to believe that his is not a special situation. He is fully aware of the source of his brooding—a succession of undiagnosed autopsies in the Chinese district last year. Whatever the cause, certain ones down there fall like flies to it; they go down before it as the Indians here are said first to have succumbed to measles—like them they must have had no antibodies for it. All men and women of a certain age and circumstance. Not unlike his. Parental disease of the heart? A pathologist smiled, and said no.

He has even been foolish enough to coin himself a secret name for it, no doubt grubbed from some submerged Graeco-Roman prowl of his boyhood. *Parentation*, or the performance of the funeral rites of parents.

By—or with—the child. He believes himself to be not merely in a personal situation, but a process—as in so many of the circumstances of life we really are. Of the dangers of this sort of thinking he is also fully aware. But he has come to it. Perhaps the process has brought him there? Yes, in the operating room, those small or larger amphitheaters where observers are allowed, any who ask him for theory, student or staff, still get a hissed "Watch!" But these days he carries us, his own amphitheater with him everywhere, its members changing or added to daily. We are that hypothetical arena to which even the lowest of humans makes his report.

The boys want him to pay them something. On the stoops of the sour night, people stand, offering their breasts passively to the cool traffic wind, sorry perhaps they are not machines. He thinks of the four of us he has approached. Only four of course, in a total staff of two hundred, but all outwardly hearty, positive, super-visory people like Berners himself, sturdy enough for a physical rehabilitation unit in a slum hospital. And each —until that spate of Chinese bodies last winter—harbor-ing at the secret dead-center of himself, his own core of child-woe. Each—Berners now posits—going to die like that, with not a cell disarranged, on the child-vine.

We are participating, he will suggest, in the *cacoethes*, or malignant death, of the species. He will say he finds it almost exhilarating, that the atom may not be our last abyss. We are humans; it would be fitting that we disappear humanly. In human agony.

In the coal-gas night, Berners copes with this enormous dream funeral, still looking at the child. Once imagined, he has had to deal with it like a man receiving by messenger a giant bouquet the size of his small house. One summons back other funerals, of smaller scope:

A family line on a summer porch, never photographed —and now dust which has escaped this greater dust. Two students he once roomed with at separate times: one stupid, saturnine and dead, the other dead and criminal. They turn their backs on him. The reverend headfather, then eighty, bending toward two novices, brought before him for flagellating themselves, who will die in next year's avalanche; all three stare at him. His own father, now a whistle and a cheroot on the alpine air.

All, all what innocents, on the far, safe side! Old-fashioned, valetudinarian deaths. From small sicknesses. But in the domesday light of this other, wouldn't the interpenetration of all suffering become clear?

He asks us to consider whether we may not now be finishing that Voyage of the Beagle which Darwin made. Ask ourselves, he says—*Have* the fittest survived? Or is this nature's quick "Price raised!" for having made that unique life-doll, an individual—as those faces he took us to see in the morgue and the Mott Street mortuaries all seemed to say? They were all middle-aged, like us. All on the edge of "a culture," no longer in the golden mean of any. Maybe those go first, he brooded, who in their lifetime have had more than one, and can no longer manage it. Or was it merely that lesser decline of the West which Berners' grandfather, a classmate of Spengler, claimed he too saw dragging its curved shadow up against the sun's curve? There the bodies lay, in what might be a Darwinian death—or only something caught from a mote in a basket of fruit. "All parents—" as that fact-fool of a social worker read out to them, "—of one or more child" —as if it was possible to the state of parent to have less than one. Berners will ask us what would be the most fitting human agony? Or a death the most Darwinian.

Would it be in a reversal of the roles between cadaver and child? Would it be—that our children become our cadavers, and we are forced to dance with them?

But he reminds us that his is only a first report, from a man of median imagination. Maybe those are the only ones to imagine it. Meanwhile, the hospitals round the world continue their search for the nonfilterable viruses, hoping to find an orderly degeneration in the ordinary tissues of men. When we listen to him, we must consider whether or not his is merely that.

What does the rotunda know?—he will say, concluding. *Man* is a rotunda. That is what it knows best.

Now he asks us to put aside scalpel, microscope, maybe even the hospital, and come outside with him, into a ward growing ever larger.

Follow him please into a group of ordinary parents, casting their nets for blame. Remember? This is a full report.

—————◆—————

He paid the boys two dollars to mind the car, promising more when he comes back. Can they stay out that late? Nodding, sitting on its prow like small boatmen soon to be lost in the dark, they watch him go.

Walking to Baba's, he already feels the usual irritation with these people who share his lot. Fools who sit in their misery as in a church. And would have let any local expert from the "Y" lead their interdenominational chorale. Who let him.

He had first seen the group's placard, all over town now, up in Boston. Yes, he admits that for him it was like the tea. An associative link. "Parent's Movement! Touch and Talk!" He had just come from Mott Street. So the card had interested him. Little cries, little clues from a flesh trying to tell us something? In the tortured street-cries vended anywhere. Why were people so hurriedly dividing their freedom into separate cells, for the man or woman in them, for the eater and the yogi in themselves, the worker and the idler, the aging and the young? While all the while, in some honeycomb cell hiding from the pathologist . . . ? A man and a woman, not paired, had joined him there, reading over his shoulder—new types for placards, elegant. Berners had left them to it. On the way out of his son's alley, he came back.

There are similar groups now all over this city. One down here, on our western edge. None on Mott Street —they resist. Berners goes to one outside his district, telling himself it's the proper scientific thing; he does it for us.

Examine carefully, Berners says, what I did by that. We are to pretend we are back in the simplest high school biologies, zoologies, being told of how the first platypus flops up out of the Australian shallows onto its first riverbank—or how a small arctic rodent, *myodus lemmus*, resembling a fieldmouse with a short tail, very prolific, makes a remarkable annual migration, to a sea. He asks us kindly to examine—while perhaps holding our breath in analogy—the actions of all *returning* animals. He pleads with us to examine everything he does from now on in a physical light. He believes we must reexamine all human action, as animal.

He went back uptown. To his old habitat.

Of all that group who waited in a rented room at the 94th Street "Y"—he didn't know they were waiting for him—five now remain, including him. Two couples who went along for a while have now departed. The Laskys without further communication. The Hatches, on a hunch returning in winter to a Lake Michigan summer-house which before sale had been in the family for four generations, had found their son and daughter there, and have since been reunited with yet another child. They have no idea why such remission should occur, but are staying there—close.

Two men, one Berners himself, and three women, have attended the group's sessions steadily this past winter. All but one happens to be living in single circumstances; he doubts this has any significance in the process, other than that these are the ones who have no mate to suffer it with. The other four in his group believe they are in a circumstance, not a process. They still believe the group helps.

They are: Jacob Taylor; married, one daughter; Rebecca Ruge, unmarried, indeterminate number of scattered children, one son remaining; Sylvia Fisher, honorably widowed, one daughter; Mrs. Mimi Killeen, deserted, twin boys.

He knew he had returned, the minute he entered that small rented meeting room at the "Y." They could any of them have been his former patients. The same tweeds, purses, rings, postures as had come to him for years, wanting newer noses, smoother skin; he had learned never to be sure, at a glance into his waiting room, of who wanted what. And down there in the last row, in her cheap black, his usual tithe in those days—the patient he would do for charity. The room was filled with their silent, clamorous need.

Taking a seat next to the woman in the back row, he listens with bent head. From the pressure of feeling around him he would have said there were fifty there. Actually there were twelve. When Berners was a boy sitting in the Evangelical church of a Sunday, he had always thought of it as a dispensary somewhat larger than his father's, where all applicants gave names, livelihood and need, pulling either at forelocks or impatient gold watches, while God at the top of the steeple doled out the calomel. Not being sick, he had never asked for anything. And being his father's son. Often, in his later student days, the clinic had reminded him of a church. And now, waiting his turn among these people already busy confessing what prior doors they had knocked on, he saw that they too were confused, no longer knowing the difference.

They were all new here, leaderless, and at the wry

suggestion of a man whose daughter was in prison, were just voting whether or not to call themselves *The Lookouts*—"Because we look out for them. We are their lookouts." All were people whose children had refused to have more to do with them. Again and again. In mimes and games and murderous language. And arts of silence. This last interested Berners. He imagined a solid line of children joining hands, turning their backs against this wailing wall. Opening his eyes, he saw the wall itself—a line of mothers and fathers made sensitive to the touch, hollow in the sphincter, leaking in the aorta, by their kids. He didn't need a steeple to see it. With open or closed eyes he could look down into those ords, that blubber, that stool.

"Why shouldn't *we* have a place to tell it?" a woman says.

The vote was six for the proposition, four against it, two, including Berners, abstaining. The name was never mentioned again.

Next to him the charity patient, on closer inspection a big bass blond behind her dead black, had identified herself to him, Mimi Killeen, legal wife of a vaudeville man. "I was his straight girl. When the twins was born he skipped." Now she worked as a cleaner, theaters mostly, and for "a few good people on Fifth."

But when it came her turn, she couldn't bring herself

to public talk. "Everybody says twins is so jolly!" she said, and stopped.

The group was ready to love her for breaking down. Berners guessed rather that she had no vocabulary for their kind of emotion. It had taken two more sessions for them to rid themselves of their first image of her— pulling one of those good-for-a-laugh double perambu- lators with the two jollies in it. In the picture she brought the twins were slim boys of twenty-eight, as flawlessly together in their pointed shoes, high cravats and long- lashed ephebe eyes, as they were in their suicide pacts, endlessly unsuccessful, except on her.

"And the telephone, my God the telephone," one man had said, taking up his turn. "Our house, we have an extension the phone company knows from nothing. My wife here has it, in the head. All night she sits up and waits for it to ring."

And at last she dials, Berners thought, walking. He knows that umbilical cord. And in the months since that night, how all the group suffer from it—the terrible symbiosis of the telephones, side by side in life, and not ringing. Or saying the unspeakable. Asking it. Those two had been the Laskys; they had disappeared.

27

But I, Berners, don't do that telephone act anymore. There *is* a progression; maybe we are getting closer to the body of it. I don't even go up there anymore, I let Jacob. That's how I save myself from it. And Jacob, letting one or the other of us visit his prison daughter, does the same.

———————◆———————

"Doctor, welcome," this man said when it was Berners' turn.

To Berners that first time, Jacob's snub phiz looked like the official busts of Socrates or the portraits of Tolstoi, in the final rogueries of their lives—that compressed Slav face with whose planes one could do nothing. Berners remembers thinking then that a daughter could never get over it. She hadn't. In this new phase the group is now in—in which they see each other's children where possible, or help hunt for them—Berners has seen her. What profile there is to the two faces, if fitted together nose over nose and tilted as in a medical photograph done to guide some impossible grafting, would dovetail at brows, lips and chins—a perfect seal. Or kiss.

"We have no leader," this man repeated. He wore a star sapphire ring down one knuckle, too small for him. "We should organize."

"Why should he do it?" a woman said. "Doctors are mortal."

If you think it over—this woman, Sylvia Fisher, said to Berners later—*parenthood brings out your theme*. She said many reasonable things, silly style, with the club-woman's inability to find her own.

That first time, he saw her merely as a pretty forty—face set deep in a gray-blond coifed head too big for the rest of her, elegant legs and the short, peculiarly obese body whose shape to Berners had the melted, almost transient look of tranquilizer fat. The worry-fat that people put on in ordinary life was more sebaceous, based on food. Chlorpromazine, Thorazine, and even some of the lesser drugs, put a watery fat on mental patients; he had seen these standing about on the wards, rocking on their ankles in uneven calm.

Raoul, put in hospital by the school for hunger strik-ing, had refused any such drugs, Berners thought rightly so, as usual getting himself into trouble with the resident staff, for half-abetting his son. And into deeper waters with the son. While, over the years since, hunger, ab-stention from the world, had become ever more sane than hospitals.

Actually, as Berners now knew, he had been wrong about Sylvia, whose fat came from the failed sexual activity of widowhood, put too soon on those pouter-pigeon bones. Why had such a woman's vanity failed her? That little domestic Pompadour with her luminous scarves and mouth, and clean, pillowy house—why didn't she get herself a man? Why didn't he, Berners, have a steady woman, or Jacob, with that wife, a girl? The group, holding onto each other in handfest all winter, had helped Berners find out.

"Doctor—" the man with the phiz said again, extending his hand— "I'm Jacob Taylor, doctor, I live in the Majestic." Later he told them his daughter "made fun" when he said that, his shrewd, beaten eyes meanwhile watching them. Except for that shrewdness, which sat on his back directing him to more and more city real estate, which in turn sat in his head like the Pole forests of his childhood—he was a plain man. The sapphire had been flung at him by the daughter, as the prison gates closed on her. "The matron started to pick it up. But I said no, I bent down for it. Like a story in the Bible, in my shoulders I felt it." His face was weatherbeaten, sick with fatherhood. "Like what's that play with the king's daughters—I gave her what I had, so now I get bitched."

"Lear." Lasky and his telephone wife sat entwined like a lover's knot, the fingers of both hands interlaced with the others. She never said anything. But if one watched her, one could hear it ringing. Eventually the two of them must have followed it.

"Yeah, Lear." Taylor, originally a contractor from

the Bronx, had given his daughter a Greenwich Village
flat with a chandelier—"You know Leroy Street? They
don't come any better, that old-New-York stuff"—and
three abortions. "She has done everything," he said, with
the grimace a man's face has when it is just barely not
weeping—a physiognomy Berners remembers from civil-
ian faces in war. The military, more released, often
weep. Months go by before Taylor was able to tell them
what his daughter is in prison for.

"I think maybe this group is too intellectual."

If they had all been lying on the "Y"'s floor, trying
to feel the earth nine stories down, Rebecca Ruge would
still have felt impelled to say that; like many people in
handicrafts (according to Baba who worked with them)
Rebecca felt herself to be the original custodian of earth-
vibes. She was easier with them after they visited her
house, a kind of mole tunnel built around a central stove
made of the brown-green clay she used for everything;
if Berners had told her that her mind resembled her
house, she would have been pleased. She was one of those
women whose last lover leaves them for the same reason
as the first. The gloomy-graceful pots she made were
to be respected rather than used; internationally famous
now, they were to be A.D. 4000's shards of us. Ranged in
rows differing only in size, they were an obsession ex-
uded like a daily egg. But she was viviparous too; she
had had half a dozen children, named for fruits and

31

flowers and scattered like seeds—and one she had clung to and suffered from. He was an intellectual.

Yet it was to Rebecca the group owed this custom of visiting each other's houses, which had so helped their peculiar union. In the end, everybody had owed everybody something. They couldn't know what Berners owed them; in what words would he tell them? And why? What he suspected might be happening to them was after all not an apocalypse. When would the human race stop thinking that its destiny, good or bad, was a burst of light?

Crossing 145th Street now, Berners reminds himself that the thin air of his own childhood, angel-imprinted at its four corners of house and village, church and school, has instilled in him that same vision, of people either assumpted or falling, always in impossible medieval positions, dangling their legs over their bas-relief heads, or arched like acrobats, from the breastbone.

Even that first night at the "Y," a young divorcee with movie-star hair had said—telling them with gusto of a group like theirs in Carmel—"On the coast it's a resurrection for everything, great." In the involved story she had told all the way to Jacob's house, the name of her child kept changing; by the time they got upstairs, she had disappeared. In the cab over, Berners had begun to suspect there was no child. Once in Jacob's living room, he found all the others had also; this had united them that evening more than anything.

"She's the midtown version of those women who steal babies from in front of Queens supermarkets—gee Jacob, after this place will you come to Harlem?"—Baba Hunter had said in her nonstop rhythm—"but looky, the bus is right outside." A silk redhead whose high-fashion dress effects were canceled out by her avid need for compliment, she knew all breeds of divorcée from being them, and spoke like a tipsheet for what smart people were onto. "*Into*," she said. And liked to be sure of people's knowing that before being into Harlem, she had lived on the Upper East Side. Her middle child, for whom Baba pathologically neglected the others, was half black, and blamed her mother for both sides. (Yet it was Baba who had lately suggested why not see each other's kids, or visit them?)

"Ah, any place is a place," Jacob had said, answering her "—even the Majestic" and behind him, even that first evening, they could hear his daughter laugh. Actually he saw himself and his life—with that one terrible exception—entirely in terms of buildings, and had only the simplest, routine pride in what he frankly called "my success." In his hatred of architects, his talk became almost interesting—"A building has to follow people." They came to know his sighs, which began

33

after five, when the deals and the dumptrucks were stilled. "Ah, you know what—we here're all *remittance* parents." He read detective stories far into the Central Park West night, he told them, when he wasn't watching the cloud formations stream over the Dakota across the street, on their way from the hi-riser he had built on the Jersey palisades, to a Lexington Avenue "package" he was scheming to acquire. To please his daughter, the construction on it would be small Japanese-style units with shifting-screen walls.

"So she's in prison, what else?" Sylvia Fisher had whispered to Berners, using the New York inflection, though she herself had been brought up mostly in Hawaii, a high-ranking army brat.

When Jacob's daughter was let out—in a later slip of the tongue he had once said "pardoned"—it was his idea that she could manage these units. "She's a smart girl, ideal for it. People like her at once."

The rest of them had hung their heads without comment, inwardly tallying all their own past placations. And Berners, who up to then had thought he hadn't placated, but had simply been what he was and changed the tune of it, marveled at the multiplicity with which his own very woe could clothe itself. Though compared to his and Jacob's concerns, the women's troubles seemed to him at first merely that—the looseleaf, paper complaints of the female world. He was to revise this; their attitudes—centuries of trivializing—had merely made it seem so.

Sylvia's daughter, a beauty who had been given "every advantage of her peer group" including marriage to wealth—"Two at the stables, a chauffeur—at twenty-nine it's *too* much," and was now a fashionable diet-wraith with a long line of miscarriages and her picture everywhere—would not see her mother, nobody professed to know why. Not even the son-in-law, who sent roses when Sylvia had an operation, then came himself, an oldish man "but good-looking," to lean over his mother-in-law's bed and tell her, "She says herself she and you never had a fuss. But she won't see you. I'm ashamed of her—I saw my mother every day till she died. But we're another generation. No, she's not disturbed or anything. And she rides. But the doctor keeps telling her to stop that beauty-stuff, or something will happen. She's too thin. My God, the thin she is isn't even beautiful."

Whereas Rebecca's son, who taught at a remote college in Maine and had an ulcer from it, never could bear her; she admitted it. She had wanted him to roll in the mud and stop thinking; at fourteen he had demanded she wear brassieres.

"Both ideas are impossible," Jacob told Berners privately. "On her, there's no line of demarcation. And on that coastline I built an army camp. All rock. No mud."

35

She was their comedian. But even against her, cheap wit like that lasted only a few sessions. Nowadays they wept to each other and were relieved. Though it changed nothing. "I'm coming not to trust to individual solutions," Berners told Jake privately—during the week there was a good deal of private talk now between members. "Against the ages, who do we think we are?"

That was a week he had gone up to Boston on the sinking arrow of premonition, not even trying the telephone. To visit his still-beloved saint. Who was blessedly still there. Who, being as he was, didn't throw his father down the stairs to the idlers watching Berners' try from below, or repudiate him in any of the ways Berners had learned from the group and its occasional visitors. Who had been content to stand there glowing from it, with the luminous skin of the fasting, receding from his father cell by cell. That cellular rejection, Berners could feel it! Of him the father, and through him, life. Which rejection had begun first, one would have to pry out as one would from a foreign organ grafted on a hopeful, intolerant body. *Ask*, Berners found himself pleading, to that rotunda, nameless as yet, which had already begun to attend him. Ask the cell its knowledge. Cells think.

Who shall I ask, he had thought, his breath rupturing. Who is there to ask? He had stood there, five-foot-eleven to the six-foot-four of this stubbornly pale boy he had grafted on life. Whom Berners still wanted to help to live. Who wanted to show Berners, his father, how to die. Eye to eye. All faces under starvation return to Christ—the cheekbones high, the mouth in its rictus toward the skeleton, in that special smile which begins to understand—what death understands. Berners wanted to ask it a question, but he didn't yet know the question. He felt that his son, now on that other side of the room to which he always retreated, was pressing him to learn how to ask it. Over the years they had long since ex-changed all ordinary ones. Afterward Berners, going over that long, motionless communion with the same fidelity memory had for love-play, would record it as the borderline, when the science in his own flesh, blend-ing with the biblical, first began to tell him something it knew.

When he went down the stairs, his son had turned away to the sink and was drinking a glass of water, giving Berners a little hope. But that day, Berners also began thinking that hope might be part of the process too. Deep in its own helix, the dying new graft must itself have a kind of hope.

Outside, the idlers let their glazed eyes pass over him —a prodigal father, not received.

Almost at Baba's now, in sight of that brownstone hung all the way to its top story with signs that catered photographs, permanent waves, insurance, and other body accessories, and on the parlor floor Baba's own sign, *Haute Couture*, Berners halted, bought a paper he had already read, a pack of cigarettes, and smoking one, leaned against a marquee. He didn't want to go in, to that family which now knew him so well. He had had his family, as serene now in their graves as they had been to one another in life; perhaps the process attacks first, or is more protracted in those who, with grandfathers in one civilization and sons in another, can remember such a serenity. Could it be that those beelike civilizations, which are coming on, will reverse the destiny in us, once again? He begs our pardon. Pardon of his amphitheater, which is larger than he thought, able to entrain itself anywhere. Pardon of those graves—for what must be to them the thinking of a miserably median son, not of their spirit, who deals only in flesh and its repair.

Back at Jacob's, that first meeting, they'd been watching him with that look he knew. *You're* the doctor. *Lead!*

"Doctors are mortal," Sylvia Fisher says again. Her husband had been one. "Here he's only one of us."

But he hasn't yet confessed, the only one who. They are his patients; it is hard for him. In his mind he applies to his son, who that very day, after Berners had placed a call at every break between operations, has picked up the phone. Has said—with an intonation Berners is hours later still going over for its degree of death, refusal, majesty—"No." And has hung up again.

"My son disapproves of me because I'm a plastic surgeon," Berners said. "Or that's how it began, with us." He tells them how through Raoul, because of him, he now rehabilitates only the worst. No more women bringing him wrinkles which should look biblical in the evening of life—to be made smooth as Formica. (Or men.) His son, shortly after entering Harvard, had sent him a copy of a Breughel—the two old women who stare out at the century—any—from the equality of faces which already contain one, tributaried deep. Yet, in the beginning of this reformation, Berners still did such things as taking the parrot nose from a Roman fifteen-year-old and sending her out into the world again like a madonna slightly chipped, or peeling away the liver-colored scar that covered a young clerk's mouth like a gag—whereupon the young man bought a racehorse with the other half of his inheritance, but still wouldn't marry. "Father—" Raoul had said, when told of this "—you took *half?*"

Whereupon Berners, to Erna's distraction, began taking in only those birth-torn or life-mutilated who couldn't pay. The war-torn still went to the military surgeons, who were getting the opportunity of their

39

lives, as they said now to each other, as they had said in 1941 in the hospital at Lievres—how could they have done so much in this war, without the precious learning experience of the last? Nowadays that sounded in his ear for what it was. "Ah, only civilians, what snobbery!" his son said—at that time, though a vegetarian, he was still eating. So Berners gives up what he can, the option of choice, and comes downtown, to work on anybody, anything. And his son, each week casting aside another grocery item as if it is a pearl, begins not eating at all.

"He keeps *me* on the lookout," Berners said to them. "Because of him, I see damage everywhere."

They are all quiet then, even Jake. But when Jacob has a maid bring snacks in, though embarrassed at this mixture of plates with emotion, they all eat. None of them, nor Berners, saw as yet that thin thread—that most of terribles, as Job said—which made all their children one. Nature's hand in this, nature's claw. They all still could eat.

Mrs. Taylor, Jake's wife, wouldn't come out to meet them.

"She's a nothing, a nice woman," he tells them. "We married at eighteen. She brings the girl eggrolls."

Which the girl throws back, like sapphires?

On the fringe of their chairs, a voice comes timidly. "You ever think—maybe that girl of yours is a nothing?"

The charity patient. They have forgotten her, in her

dead-black, and with the poor's habit, when applying for help, of preening itself as for a social occasion, and then falling mum. She should have been for the group that stage-set of poverty on which all social problems were supposed to be made plainer. She can say the un- speakable, or do it, as they will learn. But as with many on the ward, Berners notes, she lacks that formal psyche to which the rest of us have been trained. So to the end, these people remain mysterious. Owners of bodies, per- haps, in which one may more truly hunt a disease micro- biologically, and find it—in flesh.

Berners is good on the ward. Or up to then has thought so. "I'm Dr. Berners. You're Mrs.—?"

"Killeen, Mimi Killeen. I didn't mean to insult no- body."

The rest have their heads lowered. Jacob raises eyes, shrugs.

From the Laskys' corner, his burnished, prep-school voice says, "A nothing. If we could bring ourselves to say that." He lifts the hand interlocked with his wife's. "If *she* could."

"But that's what we're here for!" Sylvia. "To blame."

"Clap hands!" Jacob says. "Round the circle. She's right."

There weren't enough in the circle; who can hide? What should Berners say?—he has never blamed anyone but himself. Even if these others have done the same, he is still there under false pretenses. For he already feels, has begun to suspect—that no personal blame can be ascribed.

"Come on, Jake." Rebecca Ruge, lying on the floor on elbow and mountainous hip. One of those hostile people who like to get to the heart of things. She sits up and assumes the lotus position. "You're the host."

Jacob, opening his mouth, goes through a half dozen gestures, says choked. "She's not a nothing, no. A moron? With what she did—I could pray for it. She came on too strong in the sex. And I came on too strong for her."

"Incest?" Rebecca is gazing between her toes. "I do admire this rug."

Rebecca's no primitive, Sylvia said to Berners later. She just believes that everything should be displayed.

"Be a slob," Jake said.

"Hah. Now we're getting somewhere. Now we reveal."

Mrs. Lasky, next in line, her eyes on them, makes no move. Is she an actual mute? No, Berners thinks. The unused mouth of a mute has less muscular definition, he says; if one probes with the fingers one can literally feel the lack of language. That mouth had spoken and spoken.

"Alec's a beautiful boy," Lasky said, fiddling with his bow tie. "Surprisingly unspoiled for nowadays." Four-

teen schools have said it. "Not a psychopathic person-
ality. The four of us—he has a sister—have been analyzed
to a fare-thee-well. I'm broke from it. From all of it.
He's—accident-prone. Things happen around him. To
him. When he comes home—really quite bad things. No
one's fault. We interreact. Linda left home because of it
—she's doing all right but she doesn't visit us. If she
does, he will, she says; it'll draw him back. He hasn't
let us know where he is lately; it's quite heroic of him
really." He stopped short. Berners had the impression
this man never ordinarily spoke so much. "But in the
end," Lasky said softly, "he always lets us know."

Sylvia Fisher said—as if in a dream to other gathered
dreamers—"I spoiled her. But she spoiled me back— She
brought me gifts . . . like to a shrine. She looked like her
father. I looked like her. We were like you know *peers*."
Her blue eyes were startled; Berners observes to himself
that this is the way a human eye essentially looks when
tears cover it.

He thinks that he must begin to look at us this way.
Like at any species. Otherwise, if you see enough disease
or injuries, you are tempted to believe that the whole
world suffers these *personally*—that every other child on
the globe was clocked by his own indigenous little cancers, or stumped on a leg twisted congenitally, yet idio-
syncratic to him. Or was born with a hand you could
repair.

While all the while, its natural lot is coming to be. To lie in the mortuary grown and dead of its own lockstep humanity.

"Mr. Lasky—" Berners asked, "is your son—Alec—is he also—very thin?"

Lasky looked at him, blank. "As a matter of fact, no. That's always been his problem. Extremely fat."

"I thought she and I should split." Sylvia said. "*He* doesn't know, but I could of. She said 'Wait ma, till I do.' So I waited. 'Let's split, it's not good' I kept saying. 'A mother and a grown daughter.' So *she* married him." She looked at Berners. "Help me blame."

Baba Hunter, moving her bangles, says, "What helps, honey? I didn't make my baby black enough." She smiled at them brightly.

She's triumphant with modernity, Berners thought. An American type.

They had to wait for Rebecca. Other people's honesty made her sulky. "My son's ulcer bleeds when he's with me. But when he's with me, he makes beautiful pots."

Everybody laughed, even Berners—"But Mrs. Ruge, you *are* an intellectual"—and Baba carols in her silver, supperclub voice, "Oh, kidlings, this could be fun. What say next time we try touch!"

So that when it comes Mimi's turn, nobody much notices her colorless answer. She sits stolid, the skirt between her knees like an empty font, in one of those churches with too many of them. "My two?" They recall she is the one with the twins; she hasn't shown them the picture yet. She gives them the shrugging, slum answer. "They got bad flesh."

The ward hears it tossed among them; *their* diagnosis. The medical interviewers constantly have to write it down—the ward patients' answer when you first ask them. The amphitheater can hear it any day—no previous case study required. It's what they say.

Berners, making a note to have her bring in the babies to the clinic, is intent on his own declaration. He thinks now he might have said, 'I have no better flesh than my son.'

But Mrs. Lasky, the telephone wife had leaned forward. "Have you ever wished—?" She has a low, sweet voice. "Have you ever wanted them *dead?*"

Suddenly Lasky began struggling with his tie. He left, refusing help, and leaning on her.

They all secretly decided never to come back.

———————◆———————

He had had to force himself to go, and like tonight, was always late. This had endeared him to the parents' group without his meaning to—a doctor being that lax. Contrarily he feels his report will be palatable to us, possibly, because he is one of us, a doctor of medicine, not

a mystic, and not even one of those who have to reflect;
in his specialty the sum of the morbid conditions in a
patient is already plain, the pathology spread out for his
knife. In the parents' group he feels as he once had at
Monte Carlo, in the gaming company of people one
would otherwise never have chosen, pulled in among
them by the demonic cards. In both places he has become
the leader without meaning to. With the group, because
none there suspect they might be in a process. With us
because it is his aberration we have cautiously agreed to
pursue.

He reports that he is trying to give up his habit of
mentally addressing us—we, the imaginary amphitheater
he has made real.

As he went up Baba's gaudy stoop, he felt them over
his shoulder, the four, none from the same division of
the hospital—three men, and one woman whose female
partner didn't know she had a child boarded out with
a foster family—whom he had approached singly, secretly at the outset, and finally met with together.

"How did you find us?" Dr. Lee said.

One or two had led him to the others; misery seeks.
Gossip had helped. Twice he had made mistakes, stum-
bling on some other kind of suffering. Although he had

come to believe there must be none of it—once the multiplicity of the human picture was pushed aside—that nature itself was not at the bottom of. "Faces—" he said. "When you work on a face, there's a point when the flesh itself tells you it can't take anymore. Yours were like that."

Some of the others, all from varying morphologies, nodded. What a rubber glove could feel, the eye could sometimes see. Or what a microscope couldn't. They looked briefly at each other's faces that night in his office. And long at his. No confidences were exchanged; unlike the lay group, they weren't personal. Later that night the morgue, as was proper, had brought them to it.

To Berners, who as a boy had pored over his father's facsimile of the *Sepulcretum*—the seventeenth-century Swiss physician Theophile Bonet's study of postmortem appearances—their faces, as open to the arc lights as the dead purples and fatty waxes they leaned over, were like some classic study-to-be of twentieth-century morbid anatomy. None had commented. Meanwhile the handmaiden voice of the social worker, whose fact-finding zeal had chanced to bring Berners here, had gone round the histories of the corpses, which that day numbered six.

This worker, a man by the name of Mervyn Le Pine, had known none of the dead; their children had been older than any of his clients at the hospital. But he knew his community. He was the worker on Mei-ling. And in his conversations with Berners, of interest in his own right. Of French-British Canadian stock, Le Pine, in either of his ancestor countries, would have known his comfortable place among the civil-servant salt of the earth; here, his job placed him at the nation's breastbone, or the nation did, in consequence of which his own sternun was pinched, and his complexion greenish with social woe. Actually, he was uneasy with larger interpretations of the social system, and was shortly moving himself and family out of New York to some more northerly state, where he could be surer of being underpaid for doing good. He seemed to Berners intensely American, a man whose reverence for the facts fell short of perception, or would always steer him clear. But because of this, the case outlines he gave came through pure, as if strained through that agar in whose substance their death-reason couldn't yet be defined.

All the bodies had been émigrés, in their youth. All with "one or more children" ill or disgraced, missing or "gone the New York way." The community had made that phrase, and the connection too, he told them—not him. Le Pine had been curious enough to go for the lab reports; here they were. Plus a statistical projection—primitive, but indeed plain. After which Le Pine rested, with his air of not being a philosopher though keeping himself handy for them on reason's steps. "A disease of separation, they call it. Look at the next of kin."

The four had all shaken his hand—and gotten rid of him. Berners waited for them to do the same with him, but they hadn't. They had closed the door on Le Pine, as if the bodies were a treasure inside it. He would wonder, in the weeks to come, if these researchers ever remembered that they too, their bodies, might be part of the same.

"Funds won't be a problem," Cohen, a Rockefeller Fellow, said, when they got back to Berners' office. At his suggestion, officially they would be investigating the snail disease which came from the use of human feces as fertilizer, and could arrive in New York any day. "On an illegal entry," he said, smiling. "No disease ever arrives in this country in any other way, it seems. But all diseases are anybody's now."

Autopsy permissions had been a problem, until Dr. Lee had solved that for them. A noted Hodgkins disease man, he himself had it—"Got double coverage, you might say." Or triple. His son, twice breaking bones in a bike fall, had just been tested; as in old people, the bone had broken first, for another reason not mysterious. He had been "not at all surprised" to hear that Lasky's son was fat. Though Berners' hypothesis on the accelerated decline of the species more than interested him, Berners' ideas on the thinning or fading of its children—"Swiss poetics, worse than German"—certainly did not. "*All* degenerations would be included," he said somberly. "Nature doesn't hide." He himself was separated from his father, a rich importer who had very morbidly taken his son Wing Li's Western marriage, and uptown residence and habits. "But yes, there is a way I can arrange this in the community. So Dr. Li-Lee had become their liaison. He too had—gone back.

"No, she doesn't hide," Dirck Smitters, their microbiologist, had said. "That's why single causes are so hard to find." He believed that his own field had contributed little to the cure of disease, and would in the future do even less. "Finding the process doesn't cure it." Gossip had it that his weekly trips to California were to hunt for one of his children who had disappeared in the Haight-Ashbury district two years before. Who might be in India now, for all he knew, or Woodstock or Taos, or Cambridge, he said when he told them; he has become an expert on the stations of youth flight. "Thousands of them are missing, all over America."

But all four were refreshed, excited to their depths at the idea that a force moving behind certain human events might be *physical*. "Once *again*," Cohen said.

Though Minna their anesthesiologist, in her own country once a pathologist, a bulky girl, too beetle-browed for her shyness, said, "But that's neo-fascist, isn't it? You'll deny all the value of human thought."

Berners said, "We don't deny it. We are asking it."

To pursue itself to the end. Whatever end. He was still swaying from the emotion brought on by the acquiescence of these men, *these*, in his proposal. While they were making the physical studies, he would keep on with the group of parents he had joined—a group of ordinary people—and make his report. "But Minna is right; we must give the nonphysical every chance." He shrugged. "As usual."

Maybe it would be wisest if they all kept diaries, he told them—what would it be for medicine if all patients were required to, in terms of their disease! Like Keats and other phthisics had often almost done for T.B. Meanwhile they of course must have him preexamined. "After all, I was brought up a Christian, this may be only my fantasy; Evangelicals especially are full of it. To us Swiss, Jung himself was no surprise. To trust his own fantasy, he had to bring the whole human race into it. Maybe I am doing the same."

But they had decided—no. They had agreed with his own gloomily modest self-estimate—and with the battery of physical and psychological tests he had insisted on— if a man could be median, he was it; he would do.

"You will consider it though. That this may be my own expiatory dream."

Smitters said, "And ours. Niels, why else do you think we believe a word you said?"

So, while they and their subordinate teams continued

to enter the corpses of cells or to breed them, he would be their live control, live dreamer. And the placebo they gave themselves? Very carefully listened to. "The standard dreaming of a society has to be listened to," Cohen said. They were modern men, and knew the significance of dreams. If there were such a thing as standard dreams, they felt his were as likely to be, as any. He felt as if he had been given an award.

Outside the hospital, when they left it, the moon was still shining on the lustered streets. Low, rolling on the tile edge of an 1880 tenement, it seemed only ten feet from the caving window shadows of the shops. Men were crawling on it that very night. The biology of the race was a moon he and these men and women would crawl on—knocking, knock knock.

"Nobody's watching biology anymore," he said. "Only disease." And machines.

Cohen, a dermatologist who had studied four years in a leprosarium in Ceylon and at the moment worked with psoriasis, held his own hand up to the light. Covered with black hair, to Berners it looked perfectly healthy, the nervously graceful human power-tool, grown out of the ape. Nobody else but he knew why Cohen had joined them; his face had moved Berners to ask him to, one day finding him alone in the cafeteria at lunch. "Come with me," Cohen had said, when they were finished.

They had taken a bus uptown to a Herald Square corner, where in the midst of the passing crowds, a group of them—one thinks of them as a *species* now, one's children, Berners thinks, his bowels turning—were performing. Or believing. Berners is faithful to Raoul where he can. Though Raoul has never given him a clue to what he believes.

"Hare Krishna. Hare Rama." The naked feet slapped, fanatic bare, on Macy's pavement; the tambourines shivered tinny, with the rags they wore; the beardless boys carrying India in a cup to this corner, staring at the crowd over their own hoarse voices, have sword-swallowers' remote faces—we have swallowed *your* sword. One girl, shaking two gourds at cricket-leg angles above her head, is convulsed rhythmically waist to navel, which protrudes like a baby's; the head moving like a turkey gobbler's on the neck, is autonymous. She has tied the scant blond hair to a feather at the top of her long, patchy-scalped crown, reminding Berners of a "bird-woman" freak he had once seen at a circus, but the face below, tranced and jerked as it is, is neat, suburban schoolgirl, that chub kind, seen at the best colleges, which would never have needed to buy its features from him. But she isn't with the shoppers; she is here. Berners, watching, almost admires the century that has managed this miracle.

Cohen, at his elbow, says, "She's mine."

Two mornings later, he comes to Berners' office. "She saw me. I got this in the mail." The note, with no return address, reads, "I don't have to hate you anymore. Don't you know you have leprosy?" So Cohen, who no longer has a telephone number for her—"She used to tell me her hate, and I would hang on just to keep her there"—now simply follows her.

And in the moonlight outside the hospital, Cohen held both his hands before him, turned them hopefully over, but found them perfect. He grimaced at Berners. "*My* dream."

———————◆———————

Tonight at Baba's, Berners is the first one in. He knew where the key was, they all did—in case she is still out hunting the child, they will hold the meeting, but wait. Keys are often exchanged, at the rise of special sympathies between two members, until these shift. Rebecca has never given him hers, though she has to others. Mimi has never had any of them to the house. Sylvia has given keys to them all, never used since she never pursued her daughter except by phone; except for her job, and vacations with a sister in Texas, she was always there. Though she has the money for Europe, and a liveliness that should have taken well with people and places, the terror-shame of her daughter's rejection keeps her immobilized in the heart. Nobody has Jacob's key because of the wife. And because Jacob knows where his daughter is. Jacob has the key of the unit within the hospital annex that Berners now uses as home; sometimes when Berners came in from his office day he found Jacob there, and they would go to a restaurant. "You're all making yourselves into a family," Dirck Smitters said. "Watch out."

Did the group know, suspect a process after all?—had occurred to Berners; was there a hint of it passed with the keys?—if I die, you can get in. For there were no other overtures. In spite of clearly possible matchmates— Rebecca liked Jacob, and Berners, in another eon, perhaps that fine spring when Raoul was still at Harvard, could well have pillowed himself on Sylvia—the burden they shared had kept the sex away. We all smell of anesthetic to each other, he thought.

While in the other group, each one continued to conceive the process in terms of his or her self. Even when hunting what their humanity might doom them to, they could not seem to escape it. Minna Williams hadn't been surprised to hear the members of parents' group had found no sex impetus toward each other; she thought the species itself had likely crossed the climacteric, or was very near. "Exactly like a man or woman does. Why shouldn't the death of the race follow the same pattern men and women do, to its grave!"

She believed that a gradual loss of sex differentiation, just as in any old person, was racially imminent. "Of course you can say I think this because my friend and I don't do much in bed anymore."

Cohen said, "Not at all"—the world was fast approving the eerie reality over the old-style evidential, more and more—"Look at the streets." He told them of a pre-Druid dance he'd seen done in a British village, men in reindeer masks piping their antlered way down the hillside out of the wood onto the green where the whole town awaited them; how the dons in the crowd, prattling learnedly among themselves of the legend, had grown quiet, slanting their eyes exactly like the proprietor of the George, the baker and the dustman, watching the men deer go back. "We're entering the primal wood again. With all our gold knowledge on our heads. And there we shall lie down."

How extraordinary, Berners thought, that people of this caliber should already half-believe him! He said so. Dr. Li-Lee, whose father's body had come in for autopsy the week before, said, "Or share your dreams."

Baba, who had an "in" at fabric houses, had covered the broken-down walls here, and all the sofas, good and bad, of her marriages, with a green-white leaf pattern of enormous scale. People sat in it like fauna, and showed their temperaments, idling against a chair's jungle back, or sitting upright in the stiff fernery conversation was for them. None of the near neighbors she invited to visit the group had stayed; as black if not quite poor, they were still priding themselves that their troubles were not individual.

It took most people a lifetime to join the human race. Berners sees himself sitting in this green artifice, a tall specimen, fair, stolid except for the hands and maybe the eyes, and with the pallor now of an advancing vegetarianism; though he has never cared for the bloody Anglo-Saxon cookery, a year ago he had been as fond of a sedate European *bifteck* as any one. As a boy, just before coming over here, a neurasthenic aunt had dragged his mother all over spa-Europe, and Niels with them; he had learned early how the aging clocked their flesh and were martyr to it, sitting humbly in the midst of their own body-wires, listening. They liked to grab his pinkness to their gray selves and tell him why. Their future was missing. Yet when he thought of death in those days, as the young do, it was always romantic death. Nowadays, strain as he does against these cellular reveries, the roles seem to him reversed.

The young-in-flesh were now its sadder campaigners. Whether for the sake of its purity—or for its jump-quick poisons, he thinks suddenly—they *know* they are animals. And "beautiful," as they like to call themselves, yes beautiful in that sad hegemony. A sight nature didn't hide.

While we, the ugly optimists, closed our eyes to it. The young *show* the genetic process, the old merely die of it. And Cohen, standing in the street to catch sight of his daughter, Jacob at the prison, Sylvia at the phone, Minna secretly visiting a child who calls her "Uncle," Dr. Li holding his son as his bones fall, Dirck Smitters haring across continents, even poor Rebecca, whose son, safe at his milksop distance, bleeding away at the sight of her, has just come home to die of it—do we all really wish the tie were less, the gap more? As we are drawn, drawn back into it?

And he, Berners, who in recent weeks, though as he thins his chaps fall, looks more and more not like his father, his ancestors, but like his son.

Over the mantel there are two pictures, one painted on black velvet, in tongue pink and ochre and bluejay, the other made of silverpaper crumpled behind glass, both by the great-grandmothers of Baba, nee Betty, of Marblehead, Mass. "And both castles," Baba once said, grinning. She's a hinterland girl, born to suck at all the city sophistications its homeborn don't bother with. Not his sort.

None of them are. They are his family. He sits in their midst like a federal spy, from the amphitheater of what he and we are afraid we know. After a winter of these people, we are only our theories; they are his experience. He schemes how to bring us and them together. Tonight he wants to confess us to them. Somehow. Easy enough to tell theory about experience. But life works another way. It *knows* it lives and dies. What dream can tell it more?

Baba has a mirror in the hallway. He goes to it. Those eyes—see them not as yours, Berners, but the experienced eyes of some man whose son starves himself for a reason the son can express only in that way. The eyes, for instance, of the father of that girl who, the papers said, dwindled herself to death on a macrobiotic diet somewhere out in Jersey—if you brought *him* a dram of the evolutionary-universe described, would he drink of it?

Into the oasis behind him Sylvia Fisher steals, closing the door against the night's steam and a stray cat, and sits down, slinging a travel bag to the floor. She won't ask what he's doing at the mirror or anywhere; the group has learned not to ask.

He comes over to her. "Why don't you ask—why I'm looking at myself?" If she asks, maybe he can find the words to tell her.

"Really want to know?" She's taking off her hat and pushing back her hair; he's seen actresses do it that way in old Broadway-style plays, when they want it known they bring messages. "Because everything anyone of us does here; the others have done it too." With the least complaint of anyone here—after all, widowhood, even a thankless child, is only a common portion—her voice is the bitterest.

He sits down beside her. "Where did you go to school? You never said."

"Trained for a nurse, at Tufts. Thing to do up around Boston, then. I was sent up there. Didn't finish."

Of course, married an interne at Massachusetts General instead. Jake has to go to Boston for Berners. She won't.

"But you had for instance biology. Even zoology?"

"Probably. I can't remember. Not zo'—though my roommate did. I had Alison instead."

"But if I told you a kind of outline in such a field, you could understand it?"

"Doubt it. You forget, I work in a boutique. And Andrew always took care of things like that."

Like the income tax. Which was what most people thought the mysteries were—maybe they were right. And Andrew *had* taken care of death.

"You're going away?"

"Texas."

Summer was a bad time for the group. There were other people with grown children who were only mulling would they have the married children down to

wherever, or would the children have them? Everybody went somewhere, if only to Jones Beach. Her shop
closed for August. She was an "active" person; she had
to move life, dresses—daughters? She would rather do
the wrong thing than nothing at all.

Lately he had been forcing himself to remember that
there were those others, a great train of life on which
he and his unfortunates walked the darkened fringe.
Last Sunday he had taken himself to the happiest place
in the park, back of the old regiment house, between it
and the seal pool, where there was always a flux of new
babies, round, frilled and pied. And almost perfect, in
the golden time before differentiation—no more work to
be done on them.

He smiled all afternoon and read Darwin. Nuts-in-
May girls and striplings lean as wire sculpture cast their
silver on his pages, passing in a tincture of sweat. "Nature, if I may be allowed to personify the natural pres-
ervation of survival of the fittest, cares nothing for
appearances. She can act on every internal organ, on
every shade of constitutional difference, on the whole
machinery of life." But with extreme slowness.

From the path in front of his knees a little boy
careened, jarring Berners' book from him, was reprimanded, and joggled on, the slap he had received
echoing on down the eons of its pages. *It may be meta-*

phorically said that natural selection is daily and hourly scrutinizing throughout the world the slightest variations. The struggle for Life is most severe between Individuals of the Same Species. The path and the Sunday went on as before, vigorous and dusty, for a time. *Natural selection will modify the structure of the young in relation to the parent, and of the parent in relation to the young.* The long lilac afternoon, waning slower than any of this, pleasured him. But after a while he got up and left. A park, sad and sparkling, was always a temporary tale. His own little tragedy beleaguered him; he was impatient when it rested. He could not seem to rest it even in eternity; it was in the huff of his heart. One had to understand that about the species, he supposed. And more and more do not survive? But even Darwin, leading us in and out of the garden in the gentle calm of geology, stopped short at the extinction of us. He found those last pages of his some of the most affecting in human history—that even such a man could not believe in the end of it. Only lesser men, like himself?

"Cool in here." Sylvia was shivering.

"Baba keeps it like the South." Double windows, heavily shaded too, against the record shop yelling "Bogey! Bogey!" on the corner of Seventh Avenue, and the hot garbage lids stewing sweet-sour dinners for pickers and cats. "The white South."

"Natch. But where is she?"

"Gone to get the girl from her father's. Baba's turn."
And afraid the girl wouldn't come here straight.

"You had the kid tested, I heard."

"Yes."

"And she has it? That thing that only Negroes get?"

"Sickle-cell anemia? Oh, there're a few Sicilian cases
on record, but not over here. Yes, she has it." On the
children's ward, the patients' mothers called it The
Neemy. Like a dance.

She got up, took a candy from a bowl, then guiltily
spat it out.

"Eat it, you're thin enough." Surprisingly this was
true. She wasn't top-heavy anymore, but small, choice
and gaunt.

"Dieting a little. For down there. In Texas, being
thinner is my only superiority. So're you, Niels—thin.
Listen, Niels, I'm leaving the group. I'm going to sit and
watch my sister's appleblossom kids and not even wish
there's anything wrong with them. I'm leaving this.
Other people's grief doesn't help." She fell into a chair
and reached for the traveling bag. "Brrr, I'm cold as sin.
Vitamin C." She put a tablet in her mouth, waited,
choked, and had to take it out. "What a pig I'm being.
Is there a disease?—you can't swallow."

"Grief."

But what has been inexplicable to him all along, he will report, is that even in the worst of their grief the parents continue to be so positive about the world; it was their young who raged at it, or mourned.

Not one living species would transmit its unaltered likeness to a distant futurity. Darwin had said, signing off to his amphitheater, and of the species now living few would transmit progeny of any kind. But two sentences on: *No cataclysm has ever desolated the wide world. Hence we may look forward with some confidence to a secure future of great length.* In which all corporeal and mental endowments would tend to progress toward perfection. It always seemed to Berners that the writer of that last had grown old on the page. He imagined his son Raoul reading it.

Sylvia was watching him. When one of the group was thinking about his child, the others usually knew. "I went up to that prison," she said. "Jake's. You went for him once."

"Couple of months ago." And now, Jake had gone for him.

"He said, ask for her under the name Tomashevsky, she never would use her married one. I never thought. Taylor, he must have changed his name after. God, I never connected it. *Doris Tomashevsky*. The one who—"

Killed her own farrow. Not like a sow. Thoughtfully. After a lapse of some years.

"—her little boy and girl." She still gave it the holy intonation.

"Only way he can bring himself to tell us. By sending us."

Berners will report that this is what he likes best about the group, that they have been emissaries of one another. This seems to him biblical. Or to belong to another century, of greater breadth. "He give you a message for her?"

She nods, but doesn't say. Probably the same one Jake had given him.

"She's gone on hunger strike," Sylvia said. "She didn't tell me. The guard."

"Hunger strike!" The versions were endless. "Did she say why?"

She shook her head. "Well—one thing for Rebecca. She won't have to come anymore."

They hold their breaths for each other.

"Are we jealous?" he asks. "That her boy's dead."

"I never dare think of Alison's death. Only of mine. Sometimes I do think—what if I'd never had her? But I still always choose—" Her voice went hoarse. "I still want to carry the burden of loving, God help me to be a good masochist."

65

"They don't," he said. "The children."

Alison. Raoul. Over the distance, do they exert their soft, negative pressure?

"I won't believe that."

No, but when you do, will you begin to die of it?

"Rebecca's making herself a cinerarium," Sylvia said.

"What's that?"

"Funeral urn. She doesn't like the ones the crematoriums provide."

"I can't see her making just one." He began to laugh.

She joins him. "Terrible to laugh."

"Not at all."

Her eyes brim over. She hoots to a stop. "Death's boutique."

"I never read Darwin without laughing now," he says. "Do you know him? A life boutique. Do you know that even parrakeets and canary birds dream?"

"No. Just the name. No, I didn't."

"Marvelous books. Marvelous unfinished books."

She looks at her watch. "Who else are we waiting for? Besides Baba."

He resists his desire to say—everybody. In the long run. But how is one to tell them? Ordinary people. He could tell a patient: I can't repair *you*. But speak of the species to him, and he will think only that you are not talking about him.

"Where's Jacob?" she said.

"Visiting."

"I'm glad. I can't face him tonight."

"He's going to phone in." Off the shuttle from Boston.

"She was neat as a pin, Niels. And that trustworthy face, Jacob's face. If we'd been in a ladies' room, she'd've been the one I'd ask 'Watch my bag.' "

"Infanticide doesn't mean you steal. And thievery can mean love." He smiled at her. "*I* might steal your bag."

"Well, I wouldn't meet you in the ladies' room. . . . Niels, how thin you are. . . . You too, you're thin."

This isn't sex, but that veil of unity which descends on victims. He will report that they have all come to love each other, in the end.

"Who's Jacob visiting for?" she said, knowing.

"For—me." And after he checks in, I'll be leaving. It'll be over. "There may be another man coming in the group. A doctor too. Name of Cohen."

"You're leaving too!" she said.

"Sylvia—" How would she feel if she found her bad luck wasn't personal? How does he? "You have such intuition. Did you ever think how so many of our children, almost all of them—?"

But the door is flung back, a rush of hybrid noise

comes with it; Baba enters, leading her girl by the hand. After them Mimi, in the black that always makes her seem retinue.

When Baba, triumphantly holding the girl out to them, doesn't move, Mimi slinks past her to the most retreated chair in the fernery. They know her story, her air says. She told it once.

Baba's girl is exquisite, one of those junior poppets that the times and the streets specialize in, girls and boys who seemed to Berners to tout both sex and their narrow lack of physical channels for it, in clothes that were a few streaks of leather, twig, string. Her flesh, what there is of it, is cocoa, a full upper lip and dimpled chin, all Baba to the last ditch except for the enormous, velvety, black-woman's eyes—she should have had a mother like a good cow.

Instead Baba, and a prancy dress-designer father who has already drawn up plans for her wedding dress and sends her one-hundred-dollar hand-beaded shoes. Which she throws at Baba. Who is wearing them. Because Baba respects them for what they are, and all this borderline junk is what makes life bearable—the corally pearlglass so grainy actually under the fingers, the tissue-silver so shiny real to the touch. And because the girl won't?

But he is learning that the psychological answer, after all the fuss over it, is still only the outside of the inside. Understanding people in that way obstructs the natural observation of them. He is seeing Baba as a bird in a forest, where the painted feathers flash in leaves beaded with rain. He tries to recall how the arcaded streets of Berne, a fifteenth-century museum to others, were once just a locus of stone leaves to a boy.

"This is Adoree," Baba says, and he sees how chimp is her slung-out arm, pushed-up jaw, feral eyes slanted with maternity—all saying "Mine."

They sit in the frozen leftovers of all the talk.

This, after all the talk, is the species "them."

He can see Sylvia is embarrassed; She thinks they know too much about this girl. For decency.

The girl herself need only stand there; they get the message. Her collarbone tells them, hollowed up under a sneering stuck-out shoulder, and her navel, bellicose as an op-art eye. This is not her forest.

"Renee Adoree, hmmm," Mimi says. "That movie star." She doesn't small-talk. This is the talk she has. "Gee, I always wanted a girl."

"Dory—" Baba says, pleading. "Don't run off so quick." What does she want from the girl, a curtsy, a dance for them? They know the posture.

"Wheh the kids?" They know that posture too. Implacable blame.

"Bobbie's at the Fresh Air camp. Two whole weeks." Baba says proudly.

"Wheh Rennie?"

69

Baba, feathers down, says duller, "He won't say. But he swears he's coming in to see you. Tonight. So you stay home, doll, hah?"

They know—contradictorily—how the girl loves and defends her older brothers from Baba's cheapness. Her white brothers.

" 'f he comes. 'ee comes, ah'll cook fo' em. Soul food." She says it hungrily. But she herself is so thin Baba thought she was drugging. So they took tests. First that, then all of them. Minna's friend had done it for them. Then Cohen had double checked.

"Why do you talk that way!" Baba flashes. "She's at the New Lincoln school, she can talk like anybody."

Standing, the girl, one heel lifted, silently and rapidly drums the leg, the heel not hitting. Sitting, she probably does the same. He recalls doing it unconsciously at that age, being reprimanded for it at table. An adolescent habit—Berners has often wondered whether it is sex related. He remembers being careful not to say "Fidgeter!"—as his father had to him—to Raoul.

"Ain' nobuddy black here. That's why!"

She shouldn't have been let come, he thinks; she's not enough to blame. We'll be all bouleversé. When he thinks French, he is talking to his wife. A bourgeoise from Bordeaux, who until she died ran a typing school where she got her lovers, he saw nothing in her life or his that entitled them to a saint son.

70

She sees he is looking at her. "You the guy has the gal in the jug?"

He likes her for asking what he has. "No, I'm Dr. Berners, Adoree. How do you do?" If he's good on the ward, it's because he's cool to their adversity, not to them—a practical man, median enough not to awe. But he would fall in a blubber before those dwindling, fourteen-year-old knees—one has a scab—for what he thinks she knows. Can it be that she knows Raoul? Or of him. Of the kind like him. And her. For in Berners' dream they must all know each other, this kind of young. They would know the process. As animals once knew their places in the ark.

"Ver' well thank *you*. That big lady-man doctuh friend of yours don't think!"

"Minna talked to you?"

Baba turns on him. The group has learned this about itself too; in the end they always turn on one another. In the sinking ship of blame. "Yah, that big kind dike friend of yours at the clinic, she told her. 'Leave her be,' I told her, 'Leave her to *me!*' But she gives me the stare, and says it'll help us both to know what we're in for. I say, 'I don't want to look!'"

"Minna has a little girl she visits," Berners says.

"She take me in and lemme see the plates," the young girl says dreamily. "In the mikascope. Ah tell uh 'Done already show us 'ose V.D. ones in school. But I never

71

seen those.'" As her tongue shifts, New Lincoln accent to old, she is smiling. At Baba. "She say, 'V.D.? Oh you mean syph-i-lis.'" She twirls the word so prettily Berners suddenly remembers its origin—a shepherd youth. "She ask me, 'You had biology?' I say we had up to protozoa. 'But I wudden have the V.D.,' I tell her. 'My mumma's white. So lemme see what I got.' So she shows me. I say, 'Look at that pretty ole protozoo-ah. Right in my own blood!' She say nuh-ooh, a proto is a much later form of life. I say, 'You mean I don' have the latest thing. Mumma won't like that.' An' she say." She lowers her voice like the little actress she is. "An' she say, 'You late enough.'"

Canting her knees toward Baba, she brings out a pure trill of Harlem. "See mumma, I'm the latest thing."

The torturer is the tortured, Berners reminds himself. Every Christian knows it. We burn you for the hell we are dancing in. And the chains extend back, back. Poor Minna. He wonders about her child.

A whisper from Baba. "See, see. See what I'm into?"

Sylvia runs to her. "I see you should never have brought us here." She holds Baba's shakes. Looking at Berners. "This citadel we were supposed to have here. One sight of one of them—and it cracks. It's no different from any telephone booth."

For a long while the world to him, its night caverns and fleeces flung as far as a window or an oceanliner or a jet could show him, had still been only as wide or sheltered as a telephone booth. "No."

The door from the stoop opens hesitantly; a boy blurs in, sideways, nearest to Berners, whose heart jumps. Not Raoul, but he could be—bearded, with that same posture Berners knows so well. Not a shamble. A disdain of more than general outline—of straight outline. *Don't look smart.* Stand straight and you stand with the old guardsmen of the world.

"Rennie!"

Running into the crook of his long, gangling arm, the girl clasps him round the waist, her head in his armpit, looking up to his fringed smile. Given any thin profile and those straggle locks, they all do look alike—Raoul, who if still alive is reading the Six Theosophic Points of Jacob Boehme, or one of the other of the books which Berners too has at home in the pile of free education his son had once filially offered him—and Rennie the pusher, whose heroism is that he hasn't yet offered his little sister anything. Like Christs, they all look to Berners— not the great representations or the odd ones, but the sweet lithographs in every room of the Fathers who had taught him. What did that do to these boys, in the secret mirrors of themselves?

The telephone rings.

Berners blanches, though this is Baba's house. Sylvia too. Mimi, who is nearest, picks it up and answers in

73

her cleaning-woman's voice, "Hunter residence. The doctor? Yeah, he's here."

"Jake? . . . Oh, John. . . . It's my friend, Dr. Cohen. . . . John, you coming over? Oh. What? . . . No? naturally you don't know yet. . . . Who found it? . . . So. Yes of course I'll wait. We're all waiting." As I leave. He hangs up.

A new weariness, darker than the pendulum his son has swung him on. Why should he feel at the nadir, because they have *found*?

The girl, Adoree, clutching her brother's hand, is standing over her mother. "You're gonna phone Bobbie. You're gonna send him money to come home. For to get his tests. That's what you're gonna be into."

"Tests? What does she mean? Rennie. Rennie—you didn't."

His tremulous mouth is the same as hers. Neat ears, the curve of the head from parietal to frontal bones about the same; she stamps her children well. Five years ago just another blond prep-school boy? "I swear I didn't give him anything. I haven't brought it home. And I told them." He drew himself up straight. "Bobbie didn't get hooked around me."

"You're going to have tests too, Ren, you are." His sister's broad lips tremble too, but are not the same as his.

"Not me." His head hangs. "Tried the methadone, I told you. They say I'm not enough motivated."

74

"This isn't hash, honey. This is a real motivation. And I'm gonna make her pay for transfusions for you and Bobbie, just like she has to for me. She always gives me everything, leaves you the dawgfood." She woos his jacket lapel, as if putting a flower there. "We got a 'reditary disease."

A moan from Baba.

"A—you mean T.B.?" He shook her. "Dory hon, I told you to eat."

"You don't, much." She likes him to shake her, swings back and forth with it. "Uh-uh the lady didn't say the name of it. But it is one. And we got to bring Bobbie home."

"What's she got, for God's sake?" He's holding his belly; he can't take much, Berners thinks; their span is short.

"Niels, you tell him."

"She has sickle-cell anemia. Ever hear of it?"

"Yeah? Yeah, I think. Yeah. You mean—the Neemy? like you hear on the street?"

"That's it. She'll have to do as she says."

"But I thought—I thought only—" He shrinks inside his suit. Watching his mother. Who won't look at him. "The only ones who get it—on the street they say it only hits—" He looks about to vomit. Sylvia too. Mimi, eloquent in her black, squats righteously; that font between her knees will receive what it can.

75

"Don't you believe 'em!" The girl takes her brother's long, gray-nailed hand feverishly stroking it with her child paw. "They in cahoots. Because you dope, it don't supposed to matter. And me and Bobbie both is too much. So she choose me, like everytime. . . . Rennie . . . Rennie, ain't that it?"

The boy has to get his hand away, his darting eyes too. He has to be elsewhere, he can't wait. Shivering, he waits.

Baba raises up from her huddle. But she always makes somebody else do her bad business, Berners thinks. She's leaving it to him, to us.

The girl sits tall now, clasping only herself—Adoree. The flesh is telling her, Berners thinks. The flesh always knows the pace of its mortality, all its life. At some moment, the full person tenses, as to a bell—and knows the end of it. At some moment, a species? He watches the flesh, which has taught him it will tell us everything.

"Mumma. *Mumma*. Why it choose *me*?"

Suddenly the boy bolts. Out the door, into the crowd-rot to which this place is ever accessible. Knocking over an old umbrella stand Baba keeps there, full of broken cameras, handbags, candy boxes, toys for thieves to snatch she says, better than locking.

People are the last to leave a city, Berners thinks, not the rats. He used to love crowds too. In Europe their prim jostle, the rough, marine rocking of them here. But that was when crowds were made up of individuals; now the decaying forest smells of the shades that flit it; he fears their blind, seaward motion.

"Baby, baby—" Baba whispers. Walks to her, arms out. Wails it. "Baby, baby—I made you black enough."

The girl unclasps herself. No more hugging. She stands, arms at her sides. Baba's shining cheek is waiting, held out to her to be fondled or slapped.

An old illusion. They have a new answer.

A twig, a streak of leather goes past him. The girl is gone.

Berners gets up to peer out the window, to see is the boy's shadow still there, working at his arm. No, gone. Sylvia gets up too, even Mimi. Baba mistakes it.

"No, I'll go after her. I always have." On the way out she halts at the umbrella-stand with abstract interest, as if it held something for her, then goes on past.

———————◆———————

They waited because they waited. Or had learned each other's rhythms. It was like a dance.

"Think she'll find her," Sylvia whispers at the window. "The streets are all the same."

"You feel that too? Berners said. "Synonyms."

"They used to be different. Maybe it's our time of life."

"It's because we're waiting. If we weren't we'd never notice it. Lots of people our age don't."

"My sister. A healthy family." She sat down again and dallied with her travel-bag. "Think I'll get to Dallas? I was hoping you all'd help."

"You have a reservation, dear?" Mimi had won a trip to Bermuda once; now tours hung in her head like trophies to be won; if she had the money to do it, Sylvia said, she would have been that woman you met on every cruise, who had only one dress. And glad to be.

"In summer I can always get a standby. To Dallas."

Sylvia kicks aside the bag, leans her elbows on the coffee table, and cups her face in her hands. They lean with her, knowing her fancy like their own. Even Mimi strains to it. Moments when they wait like this with another member are the group's best, Berners thinks. We're like caryatids holding up the same stone. What does it really matter if his four other friends have found it a name?

"Easter," Sylvia says. "When I gave you the key, Niels. I didn't go. To Texas. All the way to the airport, I knew I was going to catch the shuttle to Washington, and then hire a car. I was like a drunk had to have that drink. When for two years you don't see your own daughter you spent a lifetime with. I'll knock down the door, I thought. I'll give them an opera, why not. . . .

That's what she does now she's not riding, he'd been telling me, listens to the hard-luck stories on the T.V. And at the same time I'm dreaming—I've got a dress for her. From Paris. Like a butterfly pressed flat. I stepped it down a size, but even if it doesn't fit, she'll say like she used to *Gee Sylvia, gee.* So I get there, one hour and three-quarters to the door, I could do it every weekend. And there she is, sitting in the garden. Six months along she must be. By now it's due. . . . Well, I've got my answer, I thought. That she should be like that, and never tell me. I slammed the car door, so she'd see me. And—I turned around and went back. All the way back."

"Easter Sunday. What hell holidays can be."

"I saw you in the park Sunday," Mimi said suddenly. "You were reading, so I didn't come close."

About us, I was reading about us. Supppose he said that? There was a great blank that protected man from his own experience. Even his friends preferred not to see Nature plain. Else how could they live? Yet if you saw a piece of it, as the great ones sometimes had, it would be something seen daily, maybe in the fold of a hand in a lap. In what men and women—and their children—saw every day. He felt himself lost, swimming between flesh and idea, the connection slipped, yet like any tadpole, he swam because he could. "I was reading

about a man who went on a cruise. A long, long cruise."
And came back with the history of the world. "My son
gave me the book. A whole pile of them. A year ago.
Before he began killing the world."

Suddenly it seemed to him he was tired of all relationship.

"Niels—hang on." Sylvia, who never touched people,
put her hand on him. "Jake'll come soon." She thought
he was breaking down.

"His reasons are getting to me," Berners said.
"Raoul's." For a minute he could no longer remember
in which of his groups he was. "I go to the park to see
the young ones who—who don't yet know they're in
the process. To remember that they are still in the
majority." But in every generation—if there is a process
—there would be more of the young who do know. Like
ours.

"The process. What process?"

He took her hands. "You didn't have zoology. But
you had analysis, you once said."

"Both Andrew and I." Proudly. "Four years."

He could see that Freudian nest. And how death had
broken it down. "You settled for the short span."

"What do you mean! We covered the whole range
of our lives!" .

"I settled for it too. Raoul didn't care what I was

doing, or about the money I got for it. He just thought I was blind crazy, to repair flesh." Let the crockery break, Raoul meant. Let the shards be found.

"Your boy was spoiled by having to sit out the war. And my girl—she's no chicken, she's twenty-six—from having to wait for them. Or not wait."

"Yes, he sat. And I was proud of him." But while he sat, he had time to *see*.

"That age, you ought to go with the tide. Or it shapes you anyway. I watched their parties, Niels. Walked out on them, sneaked home again. When she gave up on life, our kind of life, she had to give up on me. She married him so she could get back, that's what. And never forgave me for it."

"Wish I had a girl." Mimi's voice was as usual. Speech for her wasn't the vehicle of agony; she could never express agony socially.

"Obsession." Sylvia nods over at her like a soprano, at an alto who has done her best. "But we can only see our own. Now we've learned that, we all ought to get out."

"Yes, yes." Berners saw himself swimming, grasping at anything. "But what if all our obsessions are the same?"

"The same," she said, staring off. "I'm sorry, I just want to be alone with mine."

"I see them in a lineup," he said. "All so different, but

the same. Think of them together, that skinny lineup. We each only thought of our own. But if you think of them together—that's what people never do."

They sat with him—tallying. When he speaks, it is for them.

"Rebecca's boy, on his milk-and-custard. Baba's two, tonight. One from drugs, one from genes." *All variations, nature accepts them all.* "Jake's girl, on her hunger strike. And your girl for a while, Sylvia, on hers." For beauty, it could even take place in the name of that. "My friend Dr. Cohen has a girl—the man who just called. I saw her on the street once. And your two, Mimi—I saw them." Even those theater harlequins with their hoofer's ankle-knobs and calves. "And—mine." Raoul, sitting in the concentric alembic of his own mind. Making his father see. "Oh, for a long time, there would be the all right ones too." Will be. "Like your sister's children, Sylvia." And the halfway ones like your own girl maybe, who will be remitted. Whom the prime process—life—would rear back and save.

He raised his head as if he had heard something. "We may look forward to that." But ours would be the others, the new. "Like a starving species," he says. "The young of it." And behind them, in strict emaciation too, a line of older bodies, in a morgue.

Mimi stirs. "That Lasky one, he wasn't fat."

"You remember!" he says.

"I saw him; he came back. They lived in my neighborhood, the good part. I used to see the three of them, carrying the stuff from the supermarket. Why wouldn't he at least let them deliver? He dragged them there twice a day sometimes, the checker said. Together the three of them musta weighed a ton."

So they let him drag them his way. That's how they got rid of the telephone.

Sometimes in Berners' student days, working round the clock, coming home in the holidays to help his father, migrating from the labs to the books to the wards, and finally to the bright, operative glare of the performing rooms—and always in the end, coming up hard, hard against the knot of substance that was a patient—the very snow in the villages had turned to a mound of flesh he walked with his alpenstock, pondering its pores. Going home and back, the neat train zippered it, the surgical rails stitched, but though he rode between steeples his reveries seemed to him natural; the mystery of the flesh was what the church itself was based on—as were all his own resurrecting hopes. It had been in the time just after the heyday of the Niehans clinics, where khans and Yankees, and the rich French and British, from their members of Cabinet to their sun-dried old writers, had gone to be regenerated by injections of the unborn fetuses of lambs and other small kill, and the high possibilities of lengthened human life had gleamed

83

through the pink twilit air like the Matterhorn on a fine tourist evening; his own father, a revered local doctor, had been to the clinic at Aigle to see the work, and had never questioned it. Why should Berners be the one fated to live out, and even hear, only the darker messages? And Berners' son.

"What happened to them?" he said.

"Dint you see in the News? They gassed."

"Oh God," Sylvia said beside him. "That little sad pair."

In front of his eyes, Mimi's hand turns over on her lap. "And the boy."

In enormous, freakishly fat persons, the upper thighs took on the lines of a bear's, the padding feet also, and the eyes went lidded and glandular; as the image of the person sank, the flesh became its own sphinx. He sees the three of them, nude and paleolithic again, lumbering to seal up window after window, maybe with old, civilized cloth that no longer fitted them—rubbers, bow ties—or just some clever tape sold in reels at the supermarket. Then one huge paw, dimpled as a child's, turning on all cocks, and all three peacefully lying down. Or the father and son. Or the son, murdering their closeness. Or the mother, passing a mirror—and stirring up a last, tenderly drugged meal. And faithfully waking, alone and fasting, to her inner clock. And to her lone, domestic chore at the stove.

84

"There're always some who won't eat for the future. Or are meant not to. But when it's the young—" His voice trembled. "That bag over there, Sylvia. I suppose you have her dress in it?"

She hooted out a laugh. "Easter, when she ran back in the house—did I tell you she did that? Yes, she's having a baby. She never filled out, but you can see she's having it. Now it's due. And last night Herbert phones me—to plead. They know I'm free, August. He says if I come near I'll kill her. And it." She stares straight ahead, the eyes with their double lens of tears. "He's afraid she means she'll kill herself. 'Maybe she wants to,' I told him, 'and blame me.' Blame. She's crazy of course. They all are, we've just never admitted it. All their reasons mean the same thing. Your Raoul, and Jake's child-killer and—and your pair too, Mimi, with their weekly fake suicides." Her voice softened, toward this other-class person who is in the same social class of despair. "Rejection, sure—what kid doesn't feel it? Didn't? Or wanted out? My own brother stowed away on an Army plane, for godsakes, to join the Navy in the States. I had an affair with a beachboy at sixteen, and was shipped up there to Boston, to school. There was even hate. *All* the conventions, between our parents and us. But this —this is another country, Niels."

In another country, his sister and his sister-in-laws, the Schwester and the Schwesterin, bring his father golden plums from the Valais, bored to yawns over the old man at dinner, clucking with his mother and chafing at her, devoted and irritable, human, going through the forms. *Respect your mother!* his father had once thundered at him, and he the green atheist who had called his churchgoing mother a name—*that Jesus-lover*—had shouted down from his attic *Has she a mind that we can?* But it was different. And we remember it. "For people like us, yes, it is really another country. We were brought up—another way. We'd be the ones to feel it most. Or first."

"Uh-uh, Niels. It's pure X-ray they're pointing at us. Like it dropped from the stars. And we stand there and take it. We even want it. We're crazy too, why else did we come here? We cooperate."

"I wish Doctor Cohen could hear you." Or Smitters. Or Darwin. A process. Had she any idea what she was telling him?

"He's not coming?"

He hesitated. "Not—for himself. He wants me to—he wants to talk to me. The hospital has found a virus that interests them."

"Virus." She picked up the bag. "Let them find mine."

He saw the eons, populated like hills, behind her. And ahead. A silvered page, that a little boy jarred. "Sylvia. The child. Your girl *is* having it."

Two women sit, miles apart from each other, blood

86

close. Looking at a man. He feels their pressure, toward what? Mimi, redfaced, seems to be holding her breath; he has never seen her like this; she has nerves. Sylvia's lip corners flicker, one, then the other, like an aper of craziness. Her face slys; she has secrets. "Know what crossed my mind? Like a shot when I saw her. That I'm only forty-six. And no menopause yet. Then I buried it. Until last night. I was up all night, dreaming it. I could get inseminated. A doctor's wife, I could manage it. I could start all over again." She has dropped the bag, staring outside Baba's fernery, at the open door. "We two could be alone then—I even dreamed it was another girl. The way we always wanted to be." Her voice went to the bottom. "Without him."

Mimi let out her breath.

"I scared myself so, I called my psychiatrist. I disgusted myself. Do I want to be her?"

Side by side. "What did he say?"

"I forgot it's August. He isn't there."

Not there. Up in Boston, Jake would have knocked and knocked. Spoken to the loiterers. Or broken in. And finding, gone for the police.

"We want to be them. We'll all huddle together in the end maybe." Eons ahead or not, he could see it, and wave to it a hand that would not even be dust. "But I can't believe in our craziness. I don't believe in my son's. Oh we parents, yes, we're coarsened by life.

87

They're still pure with it. When they run from us, it's because life tells them that too. It's the flesh, not the mind, not our everlasting mind." Which I respect because it can conceive this. "It's the flesh. Giving out."

"Niels, I can't bear this." Her face worked. She touched him.

"You think I'm giving out. Well—that too." A multitude of little failures at the end. "Nothing—clinical."

She touched his hand. He grasped for hers. "In another time. But I haven't got it."

She nodded. "We'd get together over it even in bed. Our—obsessions."

"Have it artificially," he said. "And I'll father it. Synthetically." Torture, torture. He looked at her close. She could never. He would bet on it. All her pillowiness was gone. That dewy, bee-jelly push that flesh had when it was bent on doubling itself. And able. Another beauty was refining it. "You look like a Breughel."

She was scrutinizing him too. Without sex. Victim-close.

"You'll soon tire," he whispered. "Of all relationship."

"Hell is one, isn't it."

Among the Berne fathers of his boyhood, such words had been alive. He could hear their skirt-rustle. Sounds of living had been simple, but another thing. The cratchet of cooks in the kitchen, munch-talk in the refectory, the cawing and sighs in the classes and the military drilling of the multiplication tables, outside all these the garden cooing of doves. Streets were at a distance; one phone in the headfather's study absorbed all worldly messages. Bells were the framework, the clock, and even a kind of moral statement. In that air, concepts flowed freely, six inches above the head if not inside it; heaven and hell were fluid and real, and daily. Pain, and elation too, had had a more personal chance. The word "millennium," said at supper, wouldn't have caused the blink of an eye. The death of the world was not unexpected. It was understood that the inanimate was what had to be kept at bay. Infinitely strong as it was, in comparison infinitely lasting. The frailty of human flesh, outside all sin and past it, was what was known. The miracle of grace was that this strange unarmored organism, these soft beings dented in a minute by a stone, shattered at once by an ox cart or a needle, drownable by water, blown out in an instant by a gassy flavor, had so persisted in time. And in their dream that the universe was vulnerable. To them.

In Baba's fernery, the three of them sit, with this duration they can't get rid of. Even while the universe is slowly stealing it back. Berners thinks to himself— what is the most alive to all of us here, in our dreaming?

That Jake will call, with news like a needle, either way. That for Cohen a virus has been found; will this keep him from street-corner tambourines? That Smitters, who has asked us why we should be looking for one disease, is off to Burma, land of rubies, to hunt for one child. That Sylvia waits for us to get her not to Texas but to Washington. As Jake will bring some kind of Boston to me. And that Mimi, whose gaunt, chic twins had passed him on Eighth Avenue once, swinging their canes like a two-a-day act for the populace—is kept ever on the ledge of their double void, with suicide messages, last telegrams carefully delivered, that she can't even read. Only Berners, interpreting once, knows she is illiterate. Near her, Baba's princess telephone sleeps; if that impervious plastic were to be dropped in the sea like a Spanish ducat, how many decades would it take to dissolve? Meanwhile, honest beyond any truth, it purrs for us.

Something has to be said aloud, it's more than time, the silence is too much.

"The telephone is breathing for us. Better than ourselves."

But it's their hands he's looking at. His own, blunted to antisepsis with years of repairing their like. Sylvia's pair, tense but vague, losing sex to age. Mimi's, red with labor, a country girl's pluckers, going blindly down the winter-summer sheaves of circumstance; Baba had once tried to hire them. Is there any virtue at all any more in the Society of the Hand—which had once been to him the sign of human enduring? In the fold of a hand in a lap, have I seen anything?

Berners asks us to note how at that moment he is wholly in the dream, has forgotten the report. Adding that he does not apologize.

For any of them.

"It's going to ring, I can feel it." Sylvia stood up. "But not for me. For you and Mimi maybe, with more of the same." She slung the bag over her shoulder. "Remember, Mimi, you and Rebecca, that day at my house? How I said in the night I sometimes knelt down to it. Asking it to say *Washington*. And what you said?"

When Mimi doesn't answer, she crosses to her. "Never mind, Mimi, don't bother. Cheers. And I hope you get on a cruise." It is a warmer voice Berners has never heard from her. She turns to him. "She said to us, 'I won't never kneel.' " She slung the bag to the other shoulder. "She breaks me up. Do you know those boys run up *bills* for their fancy death-trips? Pills, ambulances, bloodied clothes. And she pays for it. . . . *You* break me up. Wanting the whole world to be—who knows what. For you and your son. . . . Baba, she'll end by doing it to me too. Like Rebecca did. . . . *I* break me up, don't worry. . . . And Jake? You didn't ask me the message I had to take to her. To Doris Whatshername. Just before he went up there for you, he calls me. 'Tell her—tell her the Lexington package is almost ready. Tell her I'm working for her day and night.' "

She put her hat on. Didn't push it back. All tidings brought. "We never *did* anything." On her way past Baba's umbrella stand, the phone rang.

Three grown people on the floor struggling over it, nightmare's babies of what they are. For Mimi, lunging, had begun to beat the handset against a wall. Sylvia has slid after it, her head dangerously near the blows. Berners, butting between them, is netted at the ankle by the cord, in his ear the sound of the broken connection, above him like an animal champing—Mimi, her eyes rolled up. They are all kneeling. The phone is unharmed.

They rise together, holding each other, monstrous underwater game. Of children.

"She's in sycope, Niels. Like Andrew." When they press her in a chair, they hear her powerful sucking breath, bringing up some word over and over, like a pebble they can't catch. "What, Mimi, what?"

The eyes return. The sibyl lap is gone, its knees knocked crosswise. Encircling, they arm her with themselves. The word rolls out. "*Help.*" Her teeth close.

She's seeing something her brain won't read, Berners thinks. "Give her whiskey. Over there."

"No, I'm Jehovah's Witness. We don't drink."

They had forgotten the simple social key to her.

Speech isn't for agony. But she is ashamed before him, the doctor. He knows that from the ward. Tell the nurse, the orderly who sweeps, or even downstairs at the desk, or the elevator attendant, all the way up the path to the doctor, tell anybody—but not him. They think telling him helps create the disease.

In a corner, she and Sylvia consult, then Sylvia leads her to him.

"Are you a medical doctor? . . . I did something."

"You've taken something?"

"I give it."

He is thick, tired. "Gave?" Then it hits him. In the ward too, there are those like her who push their maimed children forward a certain way. Silently. Mothers of another sort, like Mei-ling's, will flame at the slightest wrong mention, off-hint of their child's handicap—reality is disparagement. Was there any lower species which so hewed to the weak offspring, the crazed or the half-mad, as we do? Yet even with us—there are these other parents whom civilization has made unnatural. Unable to say it, except with that push forward. Bad flesh.

"You all talked *do* something. She did." Mimi pointed at Sylvia, and behind her to all Mimi's upper-class ladies. You said not to dust the jardiniere. You said—put a tablespoon fertilizer in the plant. But her sons have helped too. They have nagged her with a word and

93

finally taught her it. "Euthanasia." She says it like a prescription. "They were always at me for it. It means if you want to, the family owes you an assist."

Sylvia helps her tell him how. She has put a horde of pills on the kitchen table, neatly divided. "Street seconals I had to buy, extra. It's hard when you have to have for two." For in their mock deaths, her two boymen are never divided. She has used a scribe to write her note to them. "The gypsy woman in the storefront, I paid her." She takes pride in having paid for everything.

Is this hate in disguise, Berners wonders—for many a time he and the others have declared this pride too. Her small sociomechanical voice gives him what answer it can. "I told the gypsy, 'Say I'm sick of it. Say I'm sick of loving. Say "Go ahead." ' "

She has stayed away from the house for last night and today. "In the Grand Central ladies' room. A girl I know is the attendant there." Marching there firmly, almost willing them to do it. "Call my bluff if they want to." Then, as the hours grow, she is swayed, filled with all the wrong ways they can hurt themselves, revenging themselves on her. "Razor blades again, and leave it too long. Or the rat stuff—that way is horrible." Or set fire to a spray can and ignite themselves. She's not a woman of natural imagination. Her sons have educated her. "Once, I have my friend call. That way, if they answer, it's not me." But they don't. By the time she's due at Baba's, she's crazed for fear they've done it—but she won't go home to it. "Two jobs they did on me this summer already. Once to the hospital. Once only the police. To break down the door." They always come home to her for it. "But if I wait out here too long, maybe *they* won't wait." She knows they always half mean to. "They're just scared," she says in her teaparty tone. "Poor things, they're just scared."

Berners has his head in his hands. To him, the worst of suicide is that all who commit it must be scared. To their misery, they must add this.

"What they would like—" She clears her throat, sits up in her chair. "They want to pull me down."

Sylvia's dry voice says, "What they would like, she thinks, is for her to do it along with them. Alongside."

Berners, lightheaded, remembers food, remembers Darwin—the nineteenth century in a beard unmystical. Do the mothering-fathering cells keep time with those of the child? His own are full of doubt. Or the floating empathy that is—fatherhood.

A man appears in the doorway—Cohen. In his face they see the shambles they are. Wild hair, traveling bags, sibyls, Berners in this fernery of women, and on the floor, off the hook all this time, the beeping phone. "Ex-

cuse me." Berners rushes to attend to it, his face tele-
graphing Cohen: our joint obsession; getting Cohen's
shrugged reply: I have no number for her anymore.

"This is Dr. Cohen."

A brief, inquiring flash from Sylvia. No, no one she
knows.

"*Please*, can I call?" Despair gives some on the ward
airs, but Mimi is too accustomed to it. Huddled over the
phone like a dram-drinker, she dials. Slowly her face
diffuses hope. "A D.A., oh thank God, a Don't Answer.
When they gone and done it, they always pick up and
tell me. . . . Unless maybe I left it too long." She lays the
phone down, gently listening. It lies there, weeping.

"Why don't we go back with her?" Sylvia whispers.

"Come on everybody!"

They are ready to follow her. Passing the phone,
Sylvia dips a knee, attends to it. Like someone who
lights a candle in church.

It rings under her hand.

She picks it up, answers. Looks at him, Berners. At
once they all do. Caryatids. Who have not forgot.

On the way, his cells tell him nothing.

"Jake!" As Jake talks, Berners relays it to his circle
of responsibles. *This* is his rotunda. "Nobody—there."
They choke with him. "The place neat . . . swept to a
fare-thee-well." Fare-thee-well. Bare. "Still one picture
—that would be of the snake?" And Jake, who has no

qualms on loiterers, who hasn't passed under their stare weekly for months, has spoken to them. "He left a week ago." "How was he, how was he, Jake, did they say?" He sees their lurking, underwater looks, pimpled faintly with an interest that shakes the ash from their idleness. "Thin—" But with a—"Oh my God, Jake. Oh my—thank God." But with a knapsack.

Who dares hope here? In this rotunda that may be the world?

Mimi gives the cry.

"We're going to Mimi's, Jake. An emergency. . . . He's at the East Side Terminal, he'll follow us. . . . He knows where."

Outside, Berners says, "My car's blocks from here." And Cohen has a car, in a nearby garage. But Mimi wants a cab. To pay for it.

In it, stalled in the flickering 125th Street crosstown traffic, the long ghosts of their faces opposite him and near, these his friends and co-mourners begin to look to him like good stone statues, crowded close. He knows where this comes from—the crypts of home, where often, already without religion, he would stop in a stone church-corner anonymous with saints, or in one of the plazas alive with stone people, and feel the good, warm life of the centuries. Then the cab wobbles on, and he is alive with them in this other life. What if one becomes confused, between the millennia and this present life?

"People have tried to live in both," he says aloud. "People have tried."

Nobody asks *Both what?* The cab jogs on, carrying this miracle. After a while, Cohen says, "What was the snake?"

"A mandala, they call it." He hears Raoul pronounce it for him. A friend of Raoul's had drawn it, in that metaphysical, religious, health-science, interior decoration of the soul—which they culled from art books, swami grocery stores, or all the stores of literature, anywhere. "Underneath is printed *The Struck Snake Does Not Die Until Sundown.*" Raoul had paid the rent for one more neat month, Jake said.

"God, look at it," Cohen said, peering out. "I haven't passed here since I got back. I don't think I ever was here. Worse than where we are." He meant the hospital. "This is the worst."

The driver, who knew his own black streets, was taking a shortcut. A known street jogs; this one flew past them, never to be recovered, on its hot stoops were people with eyes like antimony, in flesh from the pyramids.

"Yes, a national disgrace." When Berners is only paying lip-service, his Swiss accent comes back on him, as Erna often notes. Erna is in Cape May now—would Raoul go there? Never. It doesn't matter. A knapsack means life.

"The whole country is a national disgrace. I'm going back."

"To where?" Sylvia has Mimi's hand. Which has hers.

"Ceylon. My leprosarium is cleaner, more decent than anything here."

"That's not true," Berners says. "There are the parks." Sylvia laughs. "And Texas."

"I promise me the wide world," Mimi says, rolling with the wheels. "If they're only alive. Just once more."

He understands how her flesh is—not knowing yet whether to droop or revive. And how his flesh may never know. But Jake said an envelope had been left for him, in the center of that alembic so carefully—childishly—drawn on the floor.

The springless cab shakes Berners unheeded; he has a white gift lodged in his breast.

"You ought to go back, Niels." Cohen says.

"Back where?"

"Europe maybe. You don't belong here. It's getting you."

Suddenly Berners knows why Cohen is here.

"Asia's still tooth and claw. But not fake."

Berners leans from the cab, feeling the whiz of air. His mother used to wet a finger to the wind, telling them how in her house as a girl they had charted and predicted their daily course by the nearby bells, swinging like buoys anchored between weather and faith. Even here, where the wild sky conspired with the buildings and was lost, this should be possible. He pulled in his head. "It's not fake here anymore. Only convulsed." If you went to the heart of the country and sat down under a maple, an apple tree, with your knapsack, wouldn't it still be so— if it was a heart? Or if you had brought one there?

"John—I don't feel any more national relationship," Berners says. Neither had Cohen nor Smitters, nor Minna, that high night in Berners office, when they had been seeing their own palaeontological death as if it went before them on a palfrey, easily. Berners had never been sure of Dr. Li-Lee. But now that a virus had been found, they all were localized again, and ashamed. Cohen had come to tell him so.

"Do you take your family, Dr. Cohen?" Sylvia.

"Not anymore. Three of the kids are in college. And —I'm separated."

"He's fleeing street corners," Berners said cruelly. More like Raoul than himself. That resemblance was progressing too.

He turns to look at Cohen, who does look ashamed. Cohen doesn't know it yet, that he too is tired of relationship. "John—that night in my office, we'll keep it between all of us, hmmm? . . . Private." And the weeks after. Beginning with the morning at the morgue, they had all kept their own counsel, anyway.

"A wild evening—" Cohen said carefully. "But when you get together men with minds like that—"

You find a virus.

Berners sighed. "One of the best in my life. But on such things one cannot report. Certainly I am not qualified."

"Lee was afraid—" Cohen coughed. "He thinks the hospital is not the place to— Or to students, publicly."

Who are upset enough. "Such things are not really reportable."

"Smitters and I—we'd like to come to your office someday, and kick the ball around. But Minna and Lee—"

"They have found a virus," Berners said quickly. "*The* virus."

"You know his boy died? Of the bone cancer."

"Ah." At such times, who wants a report like mine? And Minna is afraid. "What of Minna's child?"

"Very young, that's all I know." Cohen smiled. "She says it was an aberration. She doesn't like men sexually."

Sylvia coughs, to remind them. Mimi, swinging her head, is watching the lights; they are drawing nearer the West River.

"Well, tell them I keep to my specialty." Next Tuesday as usual. Mei-ling. "They don't have to be there."

"The whole hospital admires what you are doing

there, Niels. The rehabilitation unit will never be the same."

He didn't answer. He had a white envelope, which Jake would bring.

Cohen is staring at his own hands. "I used to be a fair man. Niels, come visit me in Ceylon."

Where he would find his leperdom, Berners was sure of it.

"Europe?" Berners says. "I was brought up Evangelical. They deny we can be saved by good works. And my son found it out. That we cannot be saved."

"You do actually believe it then. That the millennia —are speeding up?"

Sylvia leans forward. "I'd like to remind you two there's a woman here who—"

"Never mind, Sylvia. It's great of them. I never had nobody with me before." They see that tears have joined the blood on Mimi's bitten lip. The cab passes the traffic thundering to the Lincoln Tunnel and wheels west, slowing down. As it draws up in front of the house, she says, "It's raining. Alive or dead, they're home. Raining, they don't go out, it spoils their clothes." And gets out to pay.

Berners remembers he hasn't fully answered Cohen. "There are still the parks, Sundays," he says. "And this cab."

But she won't let them all go up with her. "I'll wave

from the window; it's only three flight up." She looks up at her house; they can see this habit belongs to her and it. Watch us from the window, ma. And throw us down two dimes. When you get home, boys, be sure to push the bell and shout up.

"I'll go with you, I'm a nurse." Sylvia gives him a last sharp look, and goes. He won't see her again.

"Nice woman," Cohen says. "Yours?"

"No. No." He sees that Cohen, shifting feet, is in some kind of pain. "She has the chilliness of cities in her. But that's what I liked."

"Yes, yes. This is the Village, isn't it? I'm all turned round."

"Below it, and to the west."

"Thought I recognized it. These streets. Still so full of people."

This all-night street-flitting of people, Berners respected it. It took the place of a park.

"Niels, I can't stay," Cohen says. "A corner near here, I last saw her. I'm going to run on. One last look. You never can tell."

He nodded.

"Forgive me." Cohen says. For more than this.

"Street life." Berners smiles a little. "It now seems to me entirely natural." Mimi up there. Cohen here. And himself.

"Remember now," Cohen says. "Ceylon."

Berners has already forgotten him. Jake is coming down the wet street. Waving.

"I only went to phone, Niels."

They embrace.

Jake sobs for him. "My dear friend. My dear friend, come out of the rain."

"I can't yet. She wants us to watch the window. Sylvia went up there with her."

"Sylvia? She was at the prison for me."

"She came back. To Baba's."

"Where's Baba?"

"Her girl is sick. And ran out on us."

"It doesn't get any better," Jake says, watching the rivulets on his suede shoes. "Does it. But I had such news for my girl. She's got a private phone up there; I paid graft for it! But she won't answer. Even in prison, I can't get to her."

"Sylvia says . . . Jake, Doris is on hunger strike." Berners is surprised he has remembered it.

Jake's face slants sideways. To avoid the rain.

After a while, Berners says, "They must be having trouble up there. Getting in. But she wouldn't let us come along."

"Another attempt?"

"We don't know. This time, she left them the pills."

"That's progress." He turned up his collar.

Berners thinks of his letter, in Jake's natty Norfolk

jacket, in a pocket somewhere, forgotten. Home, under
the lamp, in a last terrified communion, he would open
it. Constant Comment, with him forever. But anyway,
a gift.

"That Lexington package cost me two million of my
own. Plus commitments I'll never see the end of. She
says I do it for myself. I knew she'd outsmart me."

The rain had stopped, or their patch of it had. "Jake—"

"Yes?"

"They do it for us."

"Bloody balls, they do." Jake peers at him. "I always
wonder about you, till today. What makes you stay
out in the rain. You've got a saint, that's why. I've got
a murderess."

"We're not the same as them." That's what's got us
where we are. And them, where they are? He watched
the four windows Mimi had pointed out. Real em-
broidered curtains the boys had put up. Swiss. "You saw
his room?" He turned. A scrap, a crumb? Whatever had
last touched him.

"It was like an empty chapel. Somebody had burned
incense, once."

"Yes, he used to do that. Or a girl he had did. But
not for a long time." No girl is for a long time; no
fathers. No relationship. "Was there . . . any sign of
food?"

"Boys downstairs said he went out once in a while.

To the store. He's left the key with them. That crowd. They didn't touch the place. A wonder."

"No, he was always giving them stuff." Camera, clothes, boots, skis and his grandfather's alpenstock, most of the pictures on the walls and many books though not all. And once, piled together in the hall like the ghost of an average boy going Egyptian-style into the after-life—a sleeping bag, an antique raccoon coat, and a Goya guitar. "All the encumbrances of life, he said. As he dispensed with them."

"Couple of books still there," Jake said gruffly. "Got 'em in my bag for you."

"What were they? Happen to look at them?"

"Niels, I looked at everything." Jake put his hands on Berners' shoulders, holding close his own face. Remember me, his phiz said—I've got prisons. "One of them is that book, you know—the monkey-man. Same copy as on your desk in the office."

"He gave it to me for Christmas, the year he left school. And the other?"

"Some paperback."

During that year, his son had given him half a dozen such at first, then one or two, then nothing more. The Darwin had been a proper edition, endpapers and all, two volumes picked up in some bookshop off the Charles.

"I know—it had like my name on it, Jacob. I'll bring them both over."

"Boehme, thanks, I have it too." Raoul had underlined some words in the Berdyaev preface. " 'What is at stake is not the tears of a child in time'—"

"What, Niels?"

But a window three flights up is opening. Sylvia appears at it, is calling down to them. "They're all right. They did it, but not till a couple of hours ago—and not much. We can take care of it." She and Mimi know what to do, and are doing it. No, they don't need an ambulance, both boys had already thrown up. Mimi had made coffee; Mimi and she had been walking them up and down. Her voice came to them temperately. "In between, she's walking in between them," she said, looking down at Jake and Niels as if they were a populace. "One on each arm."

"Not the tears of a child—in time and on earth, but the suffering, temporal and eternal of a vast number of living creatures. Who have received from God the fatal gift of freedom. God knowing the meaning and consequences of this gift." Berners gabbled it like a catechism. Long ago he had memorized the words without intending to, walking back and forth with the memory of his son. Trying to take in what they might mean to a member of that freehold generation which had never been catechised. And what might be intended in them—not by Boehme alone—for him.

"Sylvia—" Jake was saying. "You went up there?"

She nodded down to him. "Come on up if you want." The rain, starting up again, carried her words soft and clear, like beads on the mist. "I'll tell you about her. While we walk."

Jake made a move, Berners with him. She stopped them. "Not Niels. Forgive her, but she's afraid because you're a doctor. They don't want to go back to a hospital." Berners shrugged, palms up, to show he understood how he would be the last one Mimi could tell it to. Sylvia left the window. Jake was already entering the house.

"Jake!"

Jake turned a haggard face Berners had never seen. Not a phiz. "Jake, my envelope."

"Oh God, sorry." He drew it from an inner pocket from that jacket, so jaunty on a suffering man, and palmed it through the rain. "Sorry. Want me to stay while you—?"

"No, No thanks."

"That's all right." His forearm was gripped. "See you later."

"Right."

Now he had it, it was like a phone call he knew would be answered. He could wait. For home. Or a cab. If he had to know—what he had to know. Down at the bottom, he was warding off a blow. Like a patient ready for an answer he knows. He could wait. The rain began to drum.

Cabs would be at the far end of the street, in the lighted slice of avenue. This was a cul-de-sac. He started walking, heard a window flung up, his name called. He turned round. Mimi was waving from her window a half-block away. Backed up against the river, her house, a five-story out of a time past and dirt incalculable, held up its old gray slates and slats to what must be dawn, or a fire on the docks. Tiny on its façade, she kept waving to him. How could dawn redden like that, behind such rain? But it was summer, the beginning of a time when people went away. Thousands were already missing.

He ran back the half-block. Until he could see her clearly, from her third story. More tears, or the rain, must have wet the dried blood on her lip, the whole lower face was a strawberry stain. She spread her arms wide, called down nothing, didn't need to. *They're all right*. He waved back.

After she closed the window and disappeared, he continued to stand there, still seeing her, with her arms spread. A gesture radiant against the glowering heavens, half-lit without thunder, that now began to rain in cloudburst all the way from Jake's Jersey Towers, sweeping in silky sheets past Berners, to Sylvia's side of town and back to him drenching his suit, running off his bared head, making him momentarily a child. In North Boston maybe raining too, and in Cambridge—haunt of his special dreaming—rainbow tears for the harlequin young. Flame, soot and ashes on this parent city. On the parent city of Boston, when its dreamer is here. Starvation of the old sort stole down his gut. Until he phones, I starve. I'll starve, until he breaks down and phones. I'll starve like him. In the retributory dream that we have of them. He bent his head and ran for a cab.

Inside it, he felt too wet to take out the envelope, imagining a message written in pencil, or even some hieroglyph that intentionally ran when water touched it, and escaped. To be forever what he would never know—of what he would never know. But what the stain on Mimi's lip was now came to him, not blood but lipstick. She never wore it, but her boys had. The three of them must have kissed and cried, and kissed. And now she was walking them, just as down the years, with razor blade at her throat, pill and stomach pump at her back, they had walked her. Like a dance. As the cab bumped and rode smooth, cobbles to macadam, making half the Rhine journey of this city, his letter rose and fell with him. When he had first been here, sent to live with yet another aunt and attend school "for the English," the avid, delighted schoolboy of those heady morning skylines had learned quickly to save the letters beside his breakfast plate for the evenings, when he would be felled like a poisoned animal, by the mysterious shaman-sickness for home. Now the letter in his breast, from his son and maybe containing only a shaman pebble or drawing, seemed to him that—a letter from home.

When he got to his own car, a small shape was dozing on the hood. The air here smelled like a bowl of bad fruit, dawning with flies. The boy's clothes have drab death on them. Berners knows he is lightheaded, sniffing autopsies everywhere, before their time. When he goes round to the front, that filbert cheek is merely asleep, curved under its high crown of stubble in the delicate anonymity of childhood. When Berners bends over, the eyes open—the expected ones. What faith they have in their own doom! As Berners, swaying, manages to pet him, thank him, meanwhile counting out a wad of small bills that won't threaten him or get him cheated, the boy points a finger, stalwart out of sleep, at the car's license. Berners has to kneel down to the frog-talk, to catch what is wanted. A doctor. For the mumma.

Ward language comes to his rescue. "Special sick? or always?"

"Mose of dee time."

The answer comes as a relief, for Berners, his insides

rubbing together for lack of blood sugar, fears he physically can't go. Knows he won't.

"Can you write? Here, write down your name and address."

The child writes. Leaning on the hood. His other fist full of dollars.

"You believe I'll come, don't you? Tomorrow night."

The child lowers his lids, sophisticate. That smile creeps out on him.

"Here, here, I'll drive you home!"

Gone.

In Berners' hand is only an address.

His only faiths are secular, Berners thought. Like mine.

Inside the car, too done in to do more than dry off, Berners, head dropping, argues with Raoul. Who if he had become the doctor his father had hoped for—and he himself had, for a time—would have gone with that boy tonight. Who, if he still is anywhere, is saying "Go now." Not with scorn, never even accusing. But with a spatial smile for this other man, this median one. Who is sitting, played out, in his car. Have pity, Raoul, the years have made me almost another species. From you. Nothing to do even with relationship. The physical years. This is what we both forgot. . . . Played out, father? But father—it was never at my game.

The car was filling with the aerial phoning of years.

Too much money—too much care? Not enough. . . .
You used me. And taught me to use you so I can't get
out of it. Leave me!—I am alone because of you. The
wanting me to be *with*. The world is too much that . . .
and it's your world. . . . I never made it . . . won't make
another . . . just for you. . . . Love me and leave me
. . . alone.

It was a song Berners had known for a long time, a
son's song, a child's. In the machine-colored shadows of
the car, he heard it over, reheard it as his own—and
pitied himself. Healing, good as blood sugar, this feeling
he had never allowed himself. Blame.

In his breast, the letter went on beating, beating him,
like a heart.

In the stalled car, Berners drowsed, exhausted. His
mind has never been clearer for his report; he is in
Switzerland. That high patch of snow and small flowers,
clearinghouse for the neuroticisms of Europe, spa for
the dry cleaning of ideas, where the assorted morbidities
which gather like age spots, could for a while be shaken
—his land of clock towers and customs classifications,
from which neutral medium the higher grotesques of the
spirit could rise again like Alps. Eagle, he flies over it, a
voyage, warning us. We, the faces of his amphitheater
are still blurred. It's not science which will kill the
dream—he calls out to us—but the dreams of men which
are killing the science—two asymmetric spurs between

which the race is rowelled, and runs on. When the two meet—that will be apocalypse.

Berners woke. Hot, sick, empty. The letter was still beating. He tore it open, laid flat the slip of paper inside, and drank the few words like a dram. They had been laid on Japanese paper, with a brush. His son had taken care over them. *Let us be the uncollected place.* Neat or precious, kind or insane, they were beautiful; he wept for them. His son had taken such care to tell him. What a man in his decline forgets. Or a species. That the truth is in the wandering.

He was grateful for the "us."

On a Friday, his "teaching" day, Dr. Berners returned to the hospital on schedule, after a trip to the old town in which he had been born, from which some obscure ancestor on the wander from it—a Berners—might have been named. He had been to see his mother's sister, at eighty-five still powerfully extant in her notorious ill health. Even as a boy he had never been bored by old people; they had seemed to him like parts of the town, old arcades in which history lay ready, not as in the bound books he was catechized on, but slippery and untrustworthy with life. Old grottoes where he might catch the true accent of what had been, down whose grates he dangled himself like magnet. Just such a place he had expected in time to become—an old niche where his own progeny would wander of a dark, bored Sunday, yawning maybe, but knocking and testing too. Surely this was part of what was meant by being "human"—which in its turn had its hint of something just past physical law.

Pain to think any of this now, with one's own child dead or wandering. Pain to Darwin at the end, a human pain?—when gazing at that great arrangement of physical life in respect to which, even under God, he could not place us beyond. Berners had Raoul's copy now, a paperback—and still found it touching that his son had given him the old, elaborate one. In both editions, some of the passages had been marked. By each of them.

Berners' old aunt had had her resonances. For him her principal one had been that she spoke of Raoul as alive, and in the framework she and Berners shared. Letting her do so, he learned through her that this too was now the past.

No other vibrations had come to him. He was in limbo on that question. Other people were exercised. To certain rites. Each morning now, Erna presented herself, red-eyed. He'd been unable to lie to her, who saw him daily. "You could go to the F.B.I."—Mrs. Krants' suggestion. Both she and Erna saw this as fitting; if either had been lost, this is what the other would have done.

"No, I can't do him that indignity. Suppose he should be alive?"

By that, did he mean he felt his son was not? He couldn't say. What he did feel—never before admitted over that long-time telephone-umbilical—was that whatever Raoul had had in his knapsack, it was now his own. Berners said it to himself daily: I will not collect. I will let us be that to each other. At last.

Later, he began to think: This way, we have a place together. Others will think it a terrible one. Yea, a dreadful, fruitful place.

In Europe, remembering Cohen's remark, he had meant to look back on himself here, though not on his fitness for it. He no longer felt it necessary to belong anywhere. But though, over there, he thought now and then of those Chinese bodies, of those other parents he had spent a winter with and their almost mythic children, of all the bodies and all the viruses, beyond which there must be a breaking-down process he was certain of—he was reluctant any longer to name it. Personal loss had made him unable. Wary that he might only be transcribing his circumstance—into a general loosening of the hold on life. Hadn't men before this, in their deaths and tragedies, dreamed that the race was following them? One day over there, he had been gripped by a desire to discuss this with old Niehans, dispenser of a reasonable longevity to those who could pay for it, and searching him out, already hearing in his own head conversations in which there might be a grotto-echo of his own father as well, had discovered that the old man, in his eighties but not attaining the age of some of his patients, had died shortly before. So much for vibrations!

Waking that morning back in Harlem, the street had been full of young beards. They were like a second coming, to be seen everywhere, even in the corridors of the hospital—but one meant not to last. The older people, these were meant to last, long enough so that the young were assured of being. That was all that was meant, that nature ever meant. Then they might die. Beneath the covering multiplicity men had made for themselves, this was the way it had always been. And might be for eons yet. While the implacable empires build. And men think it important to know whether or not they are East or West, European or American. Had he really *seen* anything? Below all this, in the physical? To lift that multiple, psychological curtain men wove for themselves, was to dream—if not to die. One man's dreaming, he thinks, walking to his demonstration. It's all special—when you get to the dream. But he is glad this is a teaching hospital.

As he walks his corridor, Dr. Berners is making his report to us. He understands now that his sentence is for life—because of a certain loss, he will always report to us. But it is a relief to him to know who we are.

In the small waiting room back of the main amphitheater, he stands, prepped, masked, ready; he is always
early here. They are waiting for the patient. But that is
correct; it is the patient who should never wait. In these
rooms for the first time since returning, he is surprised to
recall how giggly and informal destiny is, over here. In
Europe, a few weeks ago, he had refreshed himself at
certain rotundas—his old medical school, to whose com-
petence the world still came, and the courtyard, eter-
nally rounded in bell and chapel, of the good fathers—
whose roster had not fallen off. He had gone to both
places partly because he had been brought up in them,
but for another reason also. Bad flesh. What nowadays,
did they make of it? For what secretly worries him is
what he will do, or his hands or his brain—thus cor-
rupted—will, when confronted with his next piece of it.

In that respect, can he be sure he is not simply a case
of breakdown? Or one of conscience and sorrow? He
has known artist-doctors who were besieged with doubt
when away, as it were, from their desks—but he has
never been one of them and knows none in his field. A
surgeon lost his "touch" in ways appropriately physical,
in Berners' father's day often from locomotor ataxia, in
his own from alcohol. Decently letting the symptoms
obscure their disease—that the "touch" which had been
lost was confidence.

In each home place, school and hospital, he had found

both men and concepts—and method too, under its sur-
face modernities—much the same. As if the very cassocks
and surgical aprons and coifs had gone on of themselves,
with the same replica bodies under them, only the coun-
tenances being replaced. Even these he was sure could be
found in facsimile, in the hospital going back at least as
far as Aesculepius, in the good fathers well past Luther,
to the Crusades. Over there, to be found to be the same
as another, or as in times before, could still be honorable
cause for congratulation. It was only over here that when
you told a man or a woman he was the same as another,
you insulted him. Home has soothed him, there. But
his personal worry has come back with him, not to be
resolved until in a moment or so, rubber to skin, his hand
touches a hand.

He has had to come back here to find out what he is
afraid of. Holding his own hands forward for the gloves,
receiving them from that same nurse who snorts in her
nose, he identifies it. A stray edge of gauze catches on
his shaved cheek; he has always loved being masked.
Others stand similarly, in the old slouches and alerts.
The room is charged with their adrenalin. The pooled
air wash-washes its own sound. There is that odor, to
him like sapsego, or the melilot that flavors it, once used
in plasters and poultices; to the others it will be whatever smell was early used on them. He is in the medical
gambling hall. All septic reality is at bay. What he

fears is impossible; all patients are seen well beforehand, some many times. No unknown is ever brought here. What he has been afraid of is that every hand brought him will be Raoul's.

Walking forward into the amphitheater, he loiters with the others. The patient has not yet been brought up, a routine delay. Somewhere, on an elevator, in one of the incessant traffic jams of the present, he and she, old and young, lie dreaming, reassured. One man here dreams standing up. In the audience, Berners sees Smitters, back from Burma with his ruby—yes, on occasion the missing can be found. Cohen is already in Ceylon, hunting his leprosy—swinging his want of it before him like a warning bell? Berners misses him most, he was the next nearest; he is on his way to the wandering. Dr. Li-Lee is ill, terminally, but he would be the first to say not predestinedly; he has found a virus, he will die optimistically. Minna, who has come by certain dark dreams on her own—there must be thousands who have —is here after all, looking up at him devotedly. But that's because he shares her secret; he has been with her to visit her child. All four of his brief nucleus are here with him either astrally or actually—his sharers of a moonlit night. They seem to him no more than that, nor less. Colleagues, with whom he has once spent a dreaming night out. He will report that they are not us. They alone—are not us.

Always the same nurses are here, bull-necked or heart-faced, and that intern with the long, naked Adam's apple seen more often in the ministry; for thirty years Berners has seen this gangly one, and those two residents, one earnest, one glossy, and so on up through all the ladders of staff and visitors; today there is a man from the state, acting under that word states love—*rehabilitate*. After these, the second-year students are most numerous. A few now have unhygienic beards, as must often have been the case at one or the other of those earliest medical firsts here, though a picture he has of the small-town Kentucky Dr. McDowell's first recorded entrance of the serous cavity in 1809, shows none. But neither does it show that huge, heavy ovarian cyst—had the surgeon, like old-fashioned pediatricians, weighed his hand with it?—brought forth like Western medicine's first egg. In a daguerreotype Berners owns—it had hung in the uptown office—Warren and Morton, ready to perform ether anesthesia, are shown clean-shaven, but there are a few attending muttonchops. The girl on the operating table, in a white gown voluminous as a bride's, looks like Erna—who had always hated the thing. Accusing him of humor, to a Swiss a compliment, he told her, but perhaps she was right. "I guess you've been asleep, Jane," Warren reportedly said, receiving in answer, "I guess so, sir." "Are you ready for the operation?" "Yes, sir, I am ready." Whereupon he

picked up her amputated leg and showed it to her, saying, "It is all done."

Years ago, Berners, taken to see that old amphitheater
still intact at Massachusetts General, had been told this
story. He has a weakness—first shared with his grandfather—for these gawkily brutal "firsts" which always,
even now, popped up in these "pioneer" countries which
were still for some outside the first circle of the civilized.
Perhaps this has to do with his feeling for America.

Down in the front rows, it is always the young
bearded ones who appear to study him most fixedly. No
doubt at the first acupuncture some such students, with
their sparser Chinese chin-hairs, looked to the worried
performing surgeon like the First Sage. It won't matter,
Berners thinks, looking at us. You are all the same. Can
you take heart from it?

He can see that some of us are surprised that he is
back. We, the Raouls—for now that he is alone, he can
say that to himself; now that he no longer belongs anywhere. We who at times have been his sole amphitheater
—almost alone. One of us had stopped him yesterday,
saying crudely, "Heard you were staying over there?
Where you belong." For while we admire, we also re-
sent; it's in our juice, if we have it. But we're also the
ones who listen best.

Others of the older generation have expressed themselves more locally in whatever their own terms; yester-

day, at a meeting, Stichmain, of his former hospital, had said to him, "Come back to us, eh? Nothing much over there. Sorry to hear about your son." He is aware that people have heard different things. Always after a death or a tragedy, or a missing person, it's they who must be satisfied.

So, looking at poor Stichmain, whose daughter, rumored dead of an overdose, should help him understand it, Berners had replied, "My son is—where he felt he belonged."

What place is that? Where the son goes before the father does? Berners addresses his wife, who in the old biblical language has "gone before." He no longer misses her, but she is here. We put our children in the abyss of life, you and I. All of us. Our going down, our own fall, is a nothing, without them. We go down into it, with them. We think of ourselves rightly, as them.

When they begin to think of death first, ahead of life —that is when it too will begin. When more sons and daughters than not say—"No." When any race begins to die it is the child-cells that first say it. Then, gathering our syllogisms close as coats, let no father, from west to east, think of himself as the same as his child. That is where it begins.

Berners reports that he still believes in that far event so black to us. However, it has occurred to him that, in time, the dream of that dream may change us. He can't tell us more; like most of us he is median. He dreams with us.

But if we must be further satisfied on the state of his son, he can tell us. Raoul will hang forever in the niche of his father's mind. Dead, over and over, by the ordinary orthodoxies—autopsy, crucifixion by daily needles, war. Or alive, over and over alive and wandering.

Hang him on your walls; he is the uncollected place. "What have I to do with thee?" he says, turning to drink a glass of—is it hope? "Everything."

———————◆———————

From a stir at the rear, Berners sees that the patient is being brought to him. His hands tremble docilely. Will they work again on flesh? They must decide. He is a returning animal. They will decide for him. In a physical light. What can the noise of the century do for him now? He hears its machines, all beneficent here, dripping sucrose on poison, soft clean air on emphysymous gas, blood given on blood shed. Tucked out of hearing of this good, resolved place are its other mills, lethally grinding. Above him, the yielding heavens are filled with both. Who can tell now what name other than twentieth ours will have in the amphitheater of the universe? Berners, glad of the mask of goodness he wears, invokes this room of other good masks. A patient, one

of a species, a bit of our body, our flesh, is being brought
to him. He is expected to work on two of us, unrelated
to each other. For a minute he strains to recall which
of us comes first on the morning's schedule, the old one
or the young one, a parent or a child. On everything
else, his mind is clear. His hands are with Nature. They
wait.

Now Berners asks us to gather round him. He asks us
to help him make his report. We, his amphitheater, who
have been through so many changes of face, must know
by now who we are. We are all the parents and children
in a man's life story, beginning in arcades that antedate
Chinese bodies in a mortuary, and not ending with an
Adoree or Mei-ling. We are his Europe, and Cohen's
Ceylon. And this adopted country of his with its funny,
jackdaw, anagram name of U.S.—which Berners has
come back to, feeling it to be the best place for a man
who knows he does not belong anywhere.

In Europe, what he had seen was *Europe*, still with its
neat, Linnaean passion for the consecutive. If this melt-
ingpot of apple-tree centers, noble wounded mountains,
park benches and their rotting sages is telling him anything, it is that life is not consecutive, not preserved
down the geodetic ages in the thin gelee of national
strains—but radiating from all its spores, even into the
cancers of change.

Berners states that a man like him feels less at odds

here. On the dark fringe. But he is aware that he reports to all of us. Even to those in the light. He remembers how he used to visualize the creation in his childhood, Christmas chains of us since the beginning, hung out to roast in the starlight. We are all of us, falling from our first resurrection ever into the abyss, arched heel over head with our toes in our faces. And outstretched hands.

The patient is wheeled in. We are that one, too.

Berners, trembling, leans over his species. Bad flesh, good flesh, bit of both. The hand is a grown man's in its natural state, unmasked. Ready, if he repairs it, to scatter its chains past anything yet known of, to establish on yet other planets those sad streets that are its synonym. Bringing its dying, murdering seed along with it. Yes, he has seen this hand.

Berners' own hands are powerless. He can't make them rise. There's a murmur in the audience, coughs, and one laugh. Next to Berners, a nurse makes a small, kind, feeling sound.

Gather round, everyone, to help. Tell him how man moves his soul forward by slow hectares of land. Or sea or ships. Across the ages, finally into the floating air. How Death never fails to move along with him. And Hope, the giant mutant, on its other side.

Persuade him, all, how maybe in a new land, a freshly cracked air, the sperm of the uncharted physical will breed us new. So may we be tossed, whipped, made to run our span again like royal interplanetary horses—the sport of Nature, who is king. To which sport we have added hope, and all our proud despairs come of it.

Berners' hands are rising of themselves to grasp those on the table. We are all here with him; he knows who we are. We are that animal, which whether it is entering the sea of death or the ark of hope, turns equally to look back on itself. Berners and his son both have dreamed this, that they might run beneath the ark of life and see how it was moving. Along. And many a median man like him. There are always some who are enchanted with the ministries of life. He calls our attention to them. The Society of the Hand

Berners' have taken up their tools. Always at this point, he states the clinical aspects of the case, as he has been taught to do in his turn. To give direction. To the next. "We begin the surgery," he says. "Which is a relationship."

He bowed his head, and in his dream, his son anointed it.

And if this report is still Latin to you, forgive him—and the good fathers of Berne.

THIS BOOK WAS DESIGNED BY IRVING PERKINS,

THE TYPE FACE USED IS JANSON

AND THE BOOKS WERE COMPOSED BY ELECTRA COMP. CORP.

AND PRINTED AND BOUND BY THE BOOK PRESS,
BRATTLEBORO, VERMONT